I0548369

As I passed Mr. Rockhouse's study, I noticed the door was open. Mr. Rockhouse was sitting at his desk in the dark. The red ash of his cigar glowed from deep within the room like a demon snake eye. 'Anthony,' he called, 'you're fumbling through this house like a hen on Christmas. For Christ's sake, what's the problem?'

I debated whether or not I should explain my dilemma to Mr. Rockhouse. We had known each other personally for quite some time, and he is wise and very charismatic. So, I told him about Hector. The tip of his cigar blinked like a winking snake for a moment. Then he stood, turned on the light, and made his way past me. 'This isn't right,' he said, exiting down the hall, 'something is certainly bizarre here, Anthony. A dog should never survive a pointblank shot to the head from a .45. How do you explain this?'

I followed him down the hall, deeply pondering. 'He must be one tough dog,' I replied, unable to think of any more reasonable explanation.

Mr. Rockhouse made his way to his sleeping quarters. He loaded the same gun he lent me to kill Hector, checked the safety, licked his thumb, and wetted the sights. 'She's not tough,' Mr. Rockhouse said, in that know it all, Rockhouse way, 'she's made of simple flesh and bone just like me and you.'

He strolled down the hall toward the door without a worry in the world. Just before he exited the front gallery, I dared to ask him how he could explain it. 'Simple,' he said, 'it just wasn't her time to go.'

He opened the door. Hector was waiting for him there. The same dog that had growled Hell's fury to me at the laundry room window, backed away from Mr. Rockhouse, quaking with fear. Mr. Rockouse steadied his pistol and fired away. He filled Hector's body with bullets, reloaded, and fired again. Once he was satisfied Hector'd had enough, he scooped the dead dog into his arms, disappeared over the mountain, and returned an hour or so later with a triumphant smile on his face. 'Filet Mignon for dinner,' he said with that arrogant prick smirk on his lips.

We never heard from Hector again. His bones are still decaying somewhere deep in the ravine, to the best of my knowledge.

SUGARLAND
MELTING

by Sam Neace

a BlackWyrm book
Louisville, Kentucky

SUGARLAND MELTING

Copyright ©2011 by BlackWyrm Publishing

A BlackWyrm Book
BlackWyrm Publishing
10307 Chimney Ridge Ct, Louisville, KY 40299

Printed in the United States of America.

ISBN: 978-1-61318-107-2
LCCN: 2011932190

Cover design by Dave Mattingly

First edition: July 2011

Dedicated to: Everett Back, Lonnie D. Duff, Debbie Oliver, Sid Herald, Tom White, Margaret White, Price Watts, and Eli Neace. They passed away, during the writing of Sugarland Melting. I wish they could have shared this moment with me.

Acknowledgments

Rebekah Neace is the greatest thing that ever happened to me. For that, she gets my heart, soul, devotion, and sincerest thanks. I also thank her for proving wrong all of those, who said I could never marry the hottest woman in the world. My children teach me patience by testing it, but I love them more than anything, and they make me a very proud father. Paul Lewis is a brilliant writer and even better friend. Dave Mattingly and Jason Walters of BlackWyrm Publishing are true visionaries. Cris Ritchie at the Hazard Herald is a blessing to journalism in Appalachia. Randy Thompson was the first to make me feel like a real artist by banning an early draft of Sugarland Melting from www.wkcb.com. He also extended a helping hand at a desperate time in my life. His support played a major role in transforming me from blubbering idiot to articulate author. I love my in-laws, and that is something to be thankful for. One of my life's largest goals is to make my grandparents proud. If I'm just like my dad, that's fine by me. Kentucky will always be my home. Should I ever stand before the Queen of England, I will boast the majesty of Perry County and Knott County. That's where I am from, and I'm damn proud of it. Last but certainly not least, I hit my knees and humbly thank God.

First Quarter
Founding Father
1.

At the mouth of a muddy mountain, on a mid-winter's night, thirteen trailers sat arranged in the form of a cross. RJ Rockhouse stared down upon them from his house high on the hill. With old, cold breath he whispered,

"It is good."

The plumbers did plumb. The electricians did wire. The carpenters did erect. The inspectors did inspect. No one in town brought quarrel against RJ's deed. Even so, the common folk were inclined to question why.

"Why would a multimillionaire, who is ninety-nine years old, litter his acres with a baker's-dozen mobile homes?"

Even more puzzling to those about the town was the fact that Rockhouse's houses were absolutely rent-free.

"Give me your tired, your poor, your huddled masses."

Those in search of hope found it in the most unlikely of places. Rockhouse's outstretched hands welcomed the poor to Sugarland. RJ plucked thirteen families from beneath the poverty line. He could have settled for merely providing warm shelter and still been awarded a Nobel Prize. However, his helping hand did not clinch. With his own purse, he paid to provide each family with satellite television. The electric, water, trash, and telephone bills were covered by the man on the mountain. Still, his heart was not humbled. RJ wanted what they wanted. He wanted them to want no more. When Rockhouse opened his purse, businesses in town were happy to accept a piece of the pie. Thanks to the influence of RJ's money, every man, who wanted a job, was given one, and not just a job flipping burgers. Some men chose manual labor. Others chose the cozy comfort of an office. A few were granted the chance to receive higher education. RJ Rockhouse held no bias for gender. Men and women were treated equally. No longer would the children's families be branded as beggars. There were new clothes for school, a computer in each home for educational and recreational purposes, and, of course, plenty of presents under the tree. Santa Clause has nothing on RJ Rockhouse. It was not long until he realized,

"Thirteen is not enough."

So, he purchased thirty-seven more mobile homes. He plucked thirty-seven families from poverty's cold claws. Sugarland trailer park stood fifty families strong. RJ Rockhouse smiled, and everyone in town wondered why.

2.

Whispers echo in small towns. RJ Rockhouse knew that all too well. For nearly seventy-five years, he remained cocooned in his hilltop mansion, refusing to visit a barber. Men tend to gather in small town barbershops. They huddle around buzzing clippers. Their floppy Dumbo ears open wide to intercept every echo of every whisper like sonar.

"I hold no sympathy for inquiring minds," Rockhouse would say to Benjamin, his butler, "if you cannot trim my hair, Benjamin, I will let it grow from here to Heaven."

Rockhouse knew not the taste of the town diner's meatloaf. Small town waitresses are often eager to accept gossip as a tip.

"Should I desire meatloaf, I'll have Amber prepare some. I refuse to eat at the diner until the town census learns not to talk with their mouths full."

A small town will forgive a wealthy man for choosing not to eat at their greasy diner or congregate in their smoky barbershop. However, one thing a small, Kentucky town will never forgive is continuous failure to attend church on Sunday morning. Rockhouse was once a church regular. He even kept his tithe requirements, which is a lot of money coming from a man of his stature. All that came to an abrupt end. Some say he lost his faith. Others go as far as to say he devoted his life to witchcraft. For whatever reason, Rockhouse's place on the front pew remained empty for nearly seventy-five years. The pastors, deacons, and all the little lambs faces and names changed throughout the decades. The Bible, Amazing Grace, and rumors of RJ Rockhouse were all that seemed un-weathered by the shift of generations.

The last time Rockhouse's shadow stretched through the church door was the day of his wife's funeral. Those there that morning witnessed what they referred to as 'a melting.' A man, with the mental, physical, and spiritual strength of a glacier, dripped with water. Tears cut his stern features and fell into stain on his expensive, dark suit. He trickled to his knees, softened, and crumbled, until he was nothing more than a puddle, weeping and trembling on the church floor. His beloved wife lay dead at age twenty-five. Even the hardest of men would lose his stone stature, if faced with the same circumstance. RJ was a boulder. But even boulders have a melting point. God, did he grieve. (In the same church, where he pledged everlasting devotion to Jesus, as his sin stained skin splashed into baptizing holy water.)

Only five years earlier, he stood within those same sacred walls, dressed in a tux that would have wetted Cleopatra's whistle. He kissed his virgin maiden's smiling lips and swore before God and all creation that his love for her would follow him to the grave. There she was again, still smiling. And he still loved her. The same people were gathered there, but this time their palms were not slick with baby's breath. There was no Wedding March on the piano. Everyone hid grief greased faces behind praying palms. Something was wrong.

Old Lady Crenshaw curled up in the corner, hiding behind black orchid buds. RJ tried to focus through the blur of tears. Was she crying or was she laughing? Gentlemen gathered around the coffin, dressed in the traditional black coat and tie. Their paper plates bowed in the middle, heavy with greasy ham and fluffy pieces of pumpkin pie that widows had baked for the occasion. The gentlemen had the audacity to shake hands and crack jokes over Lola's dead body like she was some sort of decorative piece for them to drape their coats over or rest their coffee cups on. Black widows scurried to RJ's side, making their play on the now single, rich widower and feeding him funeral rhetoric.

"I'm so sorry, RJ..."

"She's with Jesus now, RJ..."

Their words rippled across his watery tear crest and were lost somewhere along his ridges. No words could comfort him. The glacier was gone. It had melted into mud, leaving behind a man weak as water.

RJ cowered at the widows' black toes. They stared down upon him with swollen red eyes. Their pasty white faces glowed ghostly like the moon. Black dresses smothered sunlight like death's dark veil. With fluttering fingers he clawed the widows' legs hard enough to draw blood from their shins. Some shrieked.

Some moaned sympathetically. All of them scattered. They knew what he was telling them to do and where he wanted to go. The widows had once been there themselves.

Mourners cleared a path through the aisle for RJ to crawl to his dead bride's side. He poured down the aisle like lost liquid, leaving a trail of tears the entire way. She lay on red velvet, with arms crossing her firm breasts. A crimson tide of long, soft hair splashed her shoulders. Lola Rockhouse slept amidst the clutter. The sorrowful sobs of a thousand mourners did not disturb that beauty's sleep. Her gentle face peacefully smiled, caught in the comfort of her crimson cradle. RJ squished tears from his eyelashes like a squeegee and looked around the buzzing room. All the people stared on in puzzled disbelief. Her subtle beauty had never been more evident.

Some of the gentlemen curved over Lola's coffin a little too curiously. RJ was not quite sure, but he thought he could see their lips pucker into kissing position as their eyes crossed her breasts. A few went as far as to stroke her vibrant, velvet curls with their hungry fingers.

"How dare they!"

RJ feebly crawled to Lola's side and clawed his way to her coffin's lip.

"Lola," he cried, "let's go home."

But the beauty did not awaken. Her electric, emerald eyes would not open. She was lost in Rumplestiltskin's slumber. RJ brushed a tuft of ruby hair from her tender cheek.

"You're so cold, darling," he whispered, "wake up so we can go home."

Black satin shreds and orchid petals flowed across the walls' length like melting ice cream. Mourners spit hunks of slimy ham and creamy pie- some laughing; some crying. Was this a funeral or a festival?

The mourners surrounded RJ, spinning their web of sorrow like starving spiders. They were jealous. They wanted RJ's money. They wanted his mansion. They wanted his woman.

"Get away from my wife!"

He looked down upon her. With the softness of silk, he rubbed the tip of his nose against hers. His tears splattered her eyelids. Black eyeliner cut creases down her temples and lodged like ink blots in her crimson curls.

"Are you crying, my darling?" he asked her, "don't worry. I'm here."

He wrapped his arms around his beloved Lola and lifted her from the cradle. He rocked her back and forth like he had done so many stormy nights before. His forehead kissed hers. Shimmering hair fell like flame around his face. Black tears dotted her dress.

"Come on, Lola. I'm taking you home."

He kissed her with the softness of a man lost deep in love, before hoisting her over his shoulder. Lola's dead body slumped. Stiff fingers dangled at his coat tails. Lifeless green eyes opened. Children scattered. Rows of red roses spilled to the floor. The suffocating smoke of stampeded posies arose like clouds from beneath the trampling feet of frightened children.

RJ lowered his head and plowed through the crowd. Some of them slipped and fell on carpet, moist with RJ's tears. Others grabbed at Lola, trying to steal her away.

"Keep your hands off her," he growled.

"RJ, get control of yourself..."

He held her tight. One arm wrapped her waist. The other defended his sweet lady from the circling crowd. The men tried to grasp RJ and save him from humiliation. The women hugged their children tightly, shielding their eyes from the morbid display.

RJ looked out across the crowd that called themselves his friends. Five years earlier, they showered them with rice. They wished them well. Now, however, they somehow seemed happier, knowing that RJ, who had it so easy with his millions, finally understood how it felt to be human. With their faces sculpted into stationary sadness, and the jerky movements of their black bodies, they resembled clay puppets. RJ never realized it before, but suddenly it became so apparent. The devil was pulling their strings, and if Satan had his way, lovely Lola would rot with the stinking corpses of Hell.

RJ's fist cut the crowd like Lancelot's sword. Silky strands of Lola's red hair clung to her husband's tear streaked cheeks. For the briefest of moments, RJ regained glacier strength. He knocked men, he had once called brother, chin first into tear puddles. His damsel clung tightly to her hero. Her white gown circled his shoulders like smoke. He stumbled backwards, with fist flailing blindly, until he found the church door.

"Don't you dare lay one more finger on my wife," he

threatened, opening the door, "I can destroy every one of you, and you know it. With the simple flip of my wallet, I can crush this church like a locust. I can buy up your houses and rape your land. If you desire to see the hatred in RJ Rockhouse's heart manifested, touch my wife just one more time."

Everyone backed away and stood still like a picture. Clay faces kept their sad sculpting, but the jerky movements ceased. RJ ran down the porch steps and through the yard. Lola looked out to the crowd, from over her husband's shoulder, with green, marble eyes. He made his way to the Buick, opened the passenger door, seat belted Lola, and took his place beside her at the stirring wheel. As the Buick sped away into mountain shadow, the crowd funneled through the door and wandered the yard aimlessly, moaning and shrieking like zombies. That was the last time RJ Rockhouse darkened the church door.

No one truly knows what happened next. Some perverts claim he took her home and made love to her dead body one last time. Others say he buried her somewhere in the acres of his estate. The popular belief, even to this day, is that Lola Rockhouse's body is tucked away somewhere inside his mansion. All anyone knows is that RJ Rockhouse became a recluse. Seventy-five years after Lola's passing, he had yet to be seen in town. Within a few years' time, the town folk began to notice a change. The mountain on which RJ built his gaudy mansion started... melting. Mud seeped from the peak. All the pretty red buds, dogwoods, and daisies choked and died in the sludge. Folks began to blame the sudden mud on RJ's tears.

"The man cries so much over his dead wife, the ground can't hold all the tear water."

Not a very logical theory- but then again- what else could anyone believe? Even during times of drought, the mountain kept a dark, milky coating. Mud clogged the creeks and sheeted the streets. Folks would have addressed RJ with their concern, but he remained out of sight and out of mind for seventy-five years.

Within that time period, Rockhouse had gone through seventy butlers. Occasionally, a long, black limousine would cut curves, weaving its way through town to climb the steep slope ascending Muddy Mountain. Right away everyone knew,

"RJ's hired another poor soul as his butler."

Some lasted a few years. Most made it only a day. RJ's butler of the month would venture into town once a week to check the mail and buy whatever was necessary for the house. Some butlers were young. Some were older. None of them would speak to the town folk about RJ Rockhouse or what exactly was going on inside the mansion. In fact, whenever someone asked about RJ's wellbeing, the butler faded snowy pale, begin quivering, and simply said,

"Mr. Rockhouse wishes to be left alone."

Eventually, it got to the point where the town grocer did not even quote the price to RJ's butlers. There was no need to speak to them. They would not speak in return. If the butler needed a stamp, he would ask for it. If the butler needed fresh onions, he would ask for them. You ask him nothing, especially questions pertaining to RJ.

So, the stormy night Anthony stomped into the town pub, with his boots blasting thunder and his deep blue coat beaten into black by December rain, it was only natural that all of the pub's action froze like a paused movie. Bachelors lost their breath. The bachelorettes stopped giggling. Billy's rhythm on the piano slowed like a record player with weak batteries. Joe, the bartender, stood like a fossil somehow hardened in the midst of cleaning a whiskey stained glass. The pub's doors had never opened to welcome one of RJ's butlers. This was an occasion that would forever be logged in the annals of town folklore. Everyone there knew it.

Anthony shuffled to the bar, leaving a stream of cold December through the aisle. None of the brawlers clinched their fists. None of the whores adjusted their bosoms. If he had something to say, they did not want to interrupt.

He sat on a barstool and sloshed winter water onto the hardwood floor. The cuffs of his deep blue slacks dripped muddy sludge. His tattered brown boots bled creek soot from the seams, with the rubber souls flapping like loose tongues. He had obviously walked quite a distance through the storm.

"Give me a whiskey," he wheezed to Joe, still standing dumbfounded with his wrist buried in bourbon stained glass.

Joe sat a shot glass on the bar before Anthony and filled it with the most expensive brand in the house.

"Not a shot," Anthony coughed, "give me the whole bottle."

The pub people were propped stiffly in their chairs like cardboard cutouts. They gave Joe a look that said, "For the love of God, give the man what he wants."

Joe popped the cork on a fifth of his finest whiskey and sat it by Anthony's shot glass. Whether he knew it or not, a good enough story would pay for his tab.

The people were scared of him. In fact, the very presence of anything representing Muddy Mountain frightened the people the same way a graveyard seems to intimidate folks on full moon nights. Rockhouse had gone through forty-five butlers before hiring Anthony. Anthony was no different than the rest. He was just as cold and spooky. All of RJ's butlers were as much icons of local horror as The Headless Horseman and The Grim Reaper, Anthony even more so. He managed to do what most butlers could not. He stayed with Mr. Rockhouse for over a year.

Anthony began services for RJ twenty-five years after Lola's death. By then, rumors of dark deeds in the mansion on the hill were as common as Mother Goose tales. The town's children sang jump-rope nursery rhymes about warlock RJ and his hunger for misbehaving children's blood. The adults thumbed their noses to their kid's foolish limericks but continued to lock the doors and pull the shades late at night. Of course, no one knew the truth, and they figured they would probably never know the truth, until the night Anthony dripped December poison at the beak of the local pub.

His hair shaped hard on his head, as if winter's dark clouds had opened up to rain enamel. Misshapen features jutted further from his face in pub shadow, giving him the squared appearance of Frankenstein's monster. He downed drinks of whiskey with no grimace against the gasoline taste.

"It all started with Hector," he laughed, running gnarled fingers through strands of watery hair, "that damn dog. I hated that mongrel from day one, and I thought I was smarter than him. That was my first mistake. I'm telling every one of you right now, your life will be more golden when you figure out you don't know a damn thing. None of us know a damn thing."

By now, Billy had abandoned the piano. Everyone looked straight ahead to the bar with slacked jaws dangling open. Until that moment, most of them thought Anthony was a mute. He swallowed a gulp of fiery grain and continued without stutter.

"Hector was a mutt. He knew it, too. He knew he wasn't born of a fighter's breed. That's why he prowled around late at night, when he thought I was asleep. Hector always rummaged through the garbage, sniffing out a morsel of steak. I heard his hungry panting from the window of my quarters.

He was a weak dog. His hide bore deep, purple mange scars. His nose was crooked. His teeth were corn colored. And he had only three legs. His rear right leg had been amputated, and from the looks of things, it had not been removed by any skilled veterinarian.

Sometimes I could spot him crouching near the timber, at the north end of the grounds; his snout matted with chunks of rotting green meat he had stolen from the trash, and his ears endlessly fanning the flea storm nesting on his head. The tiny splinter of bone that had once connected to knee wagged below his belly. That ignorant mutt was too stupid to realize his leg was gone. He was always trying to scratch mange bumps cracking across his belly with claws connected to paws connected to a leg that was not there."

Anthony's eyes never peeped about the pub. He was not concerned with entertaining the audience. More than likely, he would have continued his story with the same enthusiasm had there been no one else there. Anthony stared straight ahead into the mirror behind the bar like he was somehow seeing his story unfold on the glass. The audience slowly moved closer so they could hear clearly. They synchronized their movements. Whenever Anthony paused to take a shot of whiskey, they would do the same. When he lowered his voice, they leaned toward him. When he raised his voice, they tilted backwards like people dodging a darting bee. By now, Joe had waxed the whiskey stained glass to a diamond shine and continued waxing unaware, with his fascination locked on Anthony.

"I must admit, I had it out for Hector. No matter how hard I tried, he always found a way to root into the trash and spread it across the yard. I guess the dog had more brains than I gave him credit for. First, I tried poisoning him, but I swear that dog's guts were cast of iron. Finally, I'd had enough of picking through maggot infested scraps and shoveling up foul green droppings. So, I asked Mr. Rockhouse for the liberty to shoot the dog. He seemed rather keen on the idea. He loaded his .45 and handed it over to me. 'You should name it, if you're going to kill it. Does the dog have a name?' he asked.

I told him I named the dog Hector in honor of a drunken uncle, who lived with my family briefly when I was a child.

'Hector,' he chuckled, 'that's an odd name for a girl.'

I began to correct him, but decided against it. I knew Hector was a boy. I'd seen his sagging balls more times than I cared to. 'If you shoot her between the eyes, one shot is all you will need. After you kill her, bury her in the backyard. Every lady deserves a proper burial."

Had anyone else in the world wandered into the pub with this story, he probably would have lost a few teeth and more than a few dollars: not Anthony. Thus far his story had been rather bland. However, he lost not one whisper's worth of interest from the audience. They sat around him like kids cozying to a campfire, engulfed in a ghost story. This was no average Joe sharing some tall-tale about a fish he never caught. This was RJ Rockhouse's butler. They submitted unto him complete control of their inquiring minds because they knew his story was leading somewhere colder than a grave and darker than new moon midnight.

"I shot him," Anthony rasped with bourbon breath. The crowd flinched backwards, once again dodging darting bees, "right between the eyes. Hector stumbled back onto his imaginary leg and fell over deader than Lincoln. God did that dog bleed. Gallons of blood gushed from his open wound and poured across the yard. The place looked like Bunker Hill with grass painted the rusty color of fresh blood. I did as Mr. Rockhouse asked. I wrapped Hector in an old blanket and buried him in the valley.

Maybe if I hadn't seen the dog's head burst open like a rotting melon; maybe if the red blood and gray brains hadn't been so apparent against the green grass; maybe if I hadn't felt the dog's dead body grow cold and stiff in my arms as I carried him to his grave; I would have been able to find some logical explanation as to why he returned."

The audience hardened like wax figures. Their hands steadied against half empty shot glasses. Breaths were short. Muscles thickened like tar. Even the old grandfather clock propped in the corner seemed to slow the beat of its pendulum. Each time December's clouds opened, letting loose a gust of rain against the gutters, the audience jerked in their chairs and turned toward the entrance like they were expecting zombie Hector to come waddling on three legs through the pub doors.

"I was in the laundry room," Anthony continued, now gulping

whiskey with the smoothness of milk, "The night was still and warm. A storm was brewing but not yet percolating. I heard shuffling noises outside the window. My first thought was, 'a raccoon; maybe a fox.' I stood before the window looking out into the night. I saw a silhouette in the moonlight and noticed the creature was limping, but not once did I dare think it was Hector returned from the grave, until he drew close enough to the glass for me to smell his breath. There was no mistaking those dumb red eyes, and that ugly, flea bitten face. I swear to you, the bullet hole was still bleeding. A scab formed around the wound. Maggots crawled all around it. Drool dripped from Hector's green fangs, as he growled. His growl wasn't loud, but it was so fierce. It was deep and evil like something you would hear from a Hellhound, driven mad. That jaded hunk of leg bone vibrated like a jigsaw. With his snot hardened snout, he pecked the window softly, as if he were begging me to invite him in."

Bachelorettes clung tightly to their suitors' shoulders, much to the bachelors' delight. Everyone double-timed their shots of whisky and shivered with each gust of wet wind. By now, Anthony had pushed aside the shot glass and drank his bourbon straight from the bottle.

"I dashed from the laundry room and locked the door behind me. I could still hear Hector pecking the glass softly and patiently. I took a moment to gather my senses. Then the pecking stopped and I knew Hector was sniffing around the house, searching for a way inside. I burst through the mansion, checking to make sure every window and door was bolted solid.

As I passed Mr. Rockhouse's study, I noticed the door was open. Mr. Rockhouse was sitting at his desk in the dark. The red ash of his cigar glowed from deep within the room like a demon snake eye. 'Anthony,' he called, 'you're fumbling through this house like a hen on Christmas. For Christ's sake, what's the problem?'

I debated whether or not I should explain my dilemma to Mr. Rockhouse. We had known each other personally for quite some time, and he is wise and very charismatic. So, I told him about Hector. The tip of his cigar blinked like a winking snake for a moment. Then he stood, turned on the light, and made his way past me. 'This isn't right,' he said, exiting down the hall, 'something is certainly bizarre here, Anthony. A dog should never survive a pointblank shot to the head from a .45. How do you explain this?'

I followed him down the hall, deeply pondering. 'He must be one tough dog,' I replied, unable to think of any more reasonable explanation.

Mr. Rockhouse made his way to his sleeping quarters. He loaded the same gun he lent me to kill Hector, checked the safety, licked his thumb, and wetted the sights. 'She's not tough,' Mr. Rockhouse said, in that know it all, Rockhouse way, 'she's made of simple flesh and bone just like me and you.'

He strolled down the hall toward the door without a worry in the world. Just before he exited the front gallery, I dared to ask him how he could explain it. 'Simple,' he said, 'it just wasn't her time to go.'

He opened the door. Hector was waiting for him there. The same dog that had growled Hell's fury to me at the laundry room window, backed away from Mr. Rockhouse, quaking with fear. Mr. Rockouse steadied his pistol and fired away. He filled Hector's body with bullets, reloaded, and fired again. Once he was satisfied Hector'd had enough, he scooped the dead dog into his arms, disappeared over the mountain, and returned an hour or so later with a triumphant smile on his face. 'Filet Mignon for dinner,' he said with that arrogant prick smirk on his lips.

We never heard from Hector again. His bones are still decaying somewhere deep in the ravine, to the best of my knowledge."

"That's a hell of a story," one drunken brawler called from the corner. Everyone looked at him the way an audience looks at a screaming baby in the theater. To speak to Anthony would remind him he was in the midst of a crowd, and may hinder him from continuing his story. However, it mattered not. By this time, Anthony's head was warm with whiskey and his tongue was loose.

"That's just the beginning," Anthony boasted, "I was willing to dismiss the Hector incident all together. Everyone has one or two occurrences in their lifetime that makes us question whether or not the unreal can be real. What happened after that is what truly led me to this pub on this dark night, seeking the comfort of a bottle."

Anthony took another gulp of whiskey. His fifth was nearly halfway gone.

"Shortly after that, everything started to get weird. Mr.

Rockhouse would disappear into the basement and stay there sometimes for days. Coyotes began to circle the grounds late at night. This would not have been unusual had they always been there, but they hadn't. They came from nowhere not long after Hector's second death, keeping me awake all hours of the night with their demonic howls. They never scavenged the trash. They never came any closer than fifty yards or so to the mansion, but they lingered always. Their howling laughter filled the night. Mr. Rockhouse never acknowledged their existence, neither did I. I pretended everything was perfect and played the part of subservient butler, until the day Mr. Rockhouse's brother, Randy, showed up with that Chinese couple."

Anthony swallowed a mouthful of whiskey and shook his head like a wet dog. His eyes burned with bourbon, and his tone sharpened.

"Randy Rockhouse was very polite to me. And he seemed to bring out a side of Mr. Rockhouse I had never seen before. Mr. Rockhouse drank wine and cut jokes. Everything probably would have been perfect had it not been for the Chinese couple. Neither of them spoke a word of English, but they were young and in love. Their love transcended the boundaries of language.

Randy had gained some success in the real estate and cattle business up north in Chicago. He claimed he found the Chinese couple begging for pennies on the street corner, took pity on them, and hired them as his servants. They were illegal immigrants looking for a new start in the new world.

For a few days, everything was pleasant, despite the howling coyotes. Mr. Rockhouse was in a festive mood. Randy lightened the atmosphere with his humor and wit. Even the love struck foreigners seemed to add freshness to the stale mansion air.

About the third night of Randy's visit, he and Mr. Rockhouse began disappearing to the basement for hours at a time. I could feel the winds of change blow harder and harder each time the brothers crept away downstairs. Something unexplainable was going on down there. Randy changed. His humor became dark. His eyebrows slanted to an evil point. He began to smile at misfortune. I no longer felt comfortable with him.

Two weeks or so after he showed up, Randy asked the Chinese couple to join him in the basement. They obliged. At first, there was silence, then screams. Those high-pitched Chinese shrieks cut the air like shattered glass. I couldn't understand a word they were saying. Yet I understood everything perfectly. Randy stayed down there with them for three days solid. Finally, the screaming stopped. The next morning, Randy came into the mansion, sluggish and tired like a snake fresh from a feeding. Mr. Rockhouse disappeared into the basement. He also stayed down there for three days. Randy slept the entire time. There were no screams. Everything in the house stayed dead silent. Not even the coyotes dared to break the hush.

Finally, Mr. Rockhouse came from the basement. Instantly, he demanded a feast of pork be prepared. I did as instructed. Not long after, the Chinese couple clumsily climbed the stairs and made their way drunkenly through the mansion. Everything about them was different. They no longer cared to be by each other's side. They shuffled the halls like sleepwalkers with their slanted glossy eyes never focused on the floor unfurling before them. Eventually, the female made her way to the kitchen where I was preparing the requested feast. She took a seat at the table, stared straight through me with those yellow, cat eyes, and asked me in perfect English for a glass of water. There was not a hint of accent in her voice."

Anthony took another swallow of whiskey and jiggled the bottle- proud of the fact he had inhaled two thirds of the fifth without so much as a belch. The crowd shuffled uneasily in their chairs, unable to find any proper response to Anthony's mythical tale.

"I know what you might think," Anthony smiled, "perhaps the Chinese couple knew English the entire time and just chose not to speak it. Maybe all of them had disappeared to the basement to partake in an orgy or some other display of 'rich folk' entertainment. I thought that myself. That's how I remained sane through it all. But tonight something happened that I cannot deny. What I witnessed tonight, I hope none of you ever see, despite whatever criminal deeds you may have preformed.

It's been days since I last saw the Chinese couple. Maybe they're dead. Maybe they escaped. I don't know. Mr. Rockhouse has been subdued in his study. Since the incident in the basement, I haven't seen much of him. Randy, however, has been scurrying the house like a starving rat. He searches the closets. He roams the yard with a look in his eyes much like a broke dope fiend begging for loose change outside an opium den.

Finally, tonight the deaf silence broke me. It had been days since I had spoken and I needed to talk to someone. I didn't care what the topic of conversation might be. I needed companionship, the same as anyone of you. So, I asked Randy, as he paced the halls, what he thought of the mountain's coyote situation. 'I thought you'd never ask,' he said, 'you want those coyotes gone don't you?'

Naturally, I replied yes, expecting him to load a gun and go Wild West on the festering pack. Instead, he walked unarmed into the yard and began calling the coyotes the way you would call an old, familiar pet. Soon, one coyote heeded Randy's beckoning. It came to him meek as a lamb. He scratched it behind the ears. The coyote wagged its tale and licked his palm. Once Randy had gained the coyote's trust, he grabbed it firmly by the throat and flipped it over on its back. Before the animal had time to react, Randy was on his knees, holding the coyote's jaws shut. He clamped his teeth over its throat and began eating, as if the animal were delicate pudding. Blood coated his collar. The coyote twitched, but was too stunned to retaliate. After awhile, Randy arose from the coyote's throat. Blood poured from his lips like wine. He had a look in his eyes like a man fresh from good sex. 'Want a bite?' He asked me, with fur dangling from his teeth.

I didn't say a word. I didn't take the time to pack my belongings. I simply gathered together the money I had saved and made my way through the wilderness, off the mountain, and into town. Now, here I am, sharing a drink with you fine folks. I just feel fortunate my underwear is not saturated with piss. You all want to know what goes on in that mansion. Now, you know."

There was silence for a long while. Finally, a brawler spoke up.

"That's a damn fine story," he teased, "put his whiskey on my tab, Joe."

Anthony stood, downed what was left of his whiskey, and slapped a few bills on the bar.

"I'll pay for my own tab," he slurred, "I don't blame you guys for not believing my story. Hell, I saw it with my own two eyes, and I still don't believe it."

Anthony staggered out the door and washed away into cold December rain. No one ever heard from him again.

After that, everything returned to normal. Butlers came.

Butlers went. There were fat ones and slim ones, black ones and white ones. Despite race, religion, and cellulite, they all shared one common attribute. Whenever anyone asked about Rockhouse, they puckered like lemon lickers and sourly said,

"Mr. Rockhouse wishes to be left alone."

For the most part, the town folk obeyed this simple command. In seventy-five years, Rockhouse had only entertained a dozen guests. All of them shared the same story. He was very polite and generous, but made no quarrel when his company decided it was time to leave.

Fifty years after Lola's passing, RJ hired Benjamin as his butler. The two seemed to be a perfect fit. He was just as creepy as Rockhouse. The town's folk learned quickly not to query Benjamin.

He was by no means a meek man. His stone shoulders were broad, strong, and always seemed to be in more of a hurry than his cinderblock boots. Benjamin's beady black squint was sharp enough to cut diamond. His gnarled leather face made it impossible to determine whether he was thirty or fifty. He always wore black. Rusty hair receded a quarter of the way across his scalp. No words beyond what was necessary were ever offered. According to the postmaster, Benjamin had not spoken a word to her in ten years. He would shop the local grocery store and ask only bare minimum questions like,

"Where is the vinegar?"

This monotone, blunt style may not have been suited for social graces, but it was perfect for Rockhouse. Benjamin successfully remained his butler for twenty-five years. Word of Anthony's little song and dance at Joe's pub, decades earlier, still spread through town's streets like strawberry jam. So, it was only to be expected that the town folk raised an eyebrow when one year, two years, ten years dripped off the calendar and Benjamin still held steady to his post as RJ Rockhouse's little gopher.

Some dirty minds fancied them as gay lovers. Most folks, however, leaned toward the theory that Benjamin had either fallen victim to Rockhouse's vampire bite or he was just as much into witchcraft as his evil master.

Every now and then, RJ's limo sped off the mountain and through town, late into the witching hours of night. Those few folks burning midnight oil caught the glimmer of headlights against their frosty windows and peeked through the shades to see what mischief lurked the streets while everyone else was tucked tightly into bed.

Rockhouse's limo sliced fallen leaves, scattered along the road. Benjamin's blockhead floated white and large behind the windshield like a Halloween mask. Without hesitation, doors were locked and nightlights came to life all up and down the street. Hours later, the limo returned. The black outline of a figure fell flush against the rear window, as Benjamin quickly cut through town and followed the snaky road slithering up Muddy Mountain.

"Who is in that car with Benjamin? And what business do they have with RJ Rockhouse?"

Stories scattered like chill bumps all across town.

"Benjamin is Rockhouse's personal Renfield. He travels from town to town, seeking out prostitutes, homeless people, and runaways that no one will ever miss. They are seduced into the limo and taken back to the mansion. When they get there, RJ poisons them with a vampire scorpion bite. His bite numbs them and they lay there paralyzed but totally aware of what's going on. RJ slices into their skin with a scalpel and twirls their veins around the blade like spaghetti noodles. The victim wants to scream but cannot. He severs the clump of veins with his fangs and sucks blood from them the way a frat boy greedily sucks beer from a funnel. Benjamin watches from the corner, laughing with a wet trickle in his slacks. If the victims try to retaliate, Benjamin beats them into submission with his sledgehammer fists until their hair wrings with blood and their eyeballs pop from the sockets like a jack-in-the-box. Rockhouse eats everything. He boils the bones. He bakes the hair. He bags up the skin and saves it in his deepfreeze as a midnight snack."

This idea might appear irrational to most, but to the town folk the thought seemed logical. What else were they supposed to believe? RJ continued, year after year, to hermit himself in that boarded up gothic mansion. No one knew exactly what he looked like anymore. They could not claim assuredly that he was still alive. Benjamin served as a direct link to Rockhouse, but he was as useless as a cadaver. He hobbled around town- mumbling, drooling, and scaring little kids into therapy with his hollow eyes.

Midnight shivers became the town standard for many, many

decades, until something beautiful skipped into town from off Muddy Mountain. In many ways, the beautiful thing was more frightening than the ugly things because it was so unexpected. RJ had gone through fifty butlers. However, in all that time, he never hired a maid. Then Amber appeared.

Amber showed up on the town streets sixty-five years after Lola's funeral, much to the town folks' surprise. No long limousine announced her arrival. Benjamin, of course, had not spoken a word of her presence. She seemed to appear from out of nowhere; not that the men were complaining. Amber had thick strawberry hair and a smile that could melt a marine. Her tight butt wiggled as she giggled. She was such a contrast to Benjamin's and Rockhouse's gloomy demeanor. She cut through Muddy Mountain's ghostly fog like a light shining from a place that had been dark forever.

Everything about her shined. She glowed with a youthful carelessness that made every man either want to pinch her cheeks, pin her to the sheets, or both. The first time she danced out of Rockhouse's limo into the department store, the clerk hesitated for a moment then took a chance and asked her,

"What's your name, young lady?"

"Amber," she giggled.

"What's your last name?"

She rolled her lime eyes.

"Rockhouse, silly bones."

"Are you married to RJ?"

"Oh my God," she squealed, "yuk!"

Amber was, for some reason, permitted to do what no one else had ever been given liberty. She talked to the town folk about RJ. He was not 'Mr. Rockhouse' to her. Instead, she used names like Big Daddy, and- yes it's true- she sometimes called him 'Old Codger.' Amber shared warmhearted stories that transformed bats into butterflies. Never did she mention coyotes, or bloodsucking vampires, or dogs returned from the dead. Life on Muddy Mountain was like 'Little House on the Prairie,' according to her.

Every couple of weeks, Benjamin drove her off the hill in a limo. He opened the door for her, and she gave him a wet kiss on the cheek and smiled like Benjamin was the sweetest thing since sugarcane. Amber visited the local department store in hopes of a new doll. Naturally, the store clerk had one set aside for her.

She always totted enough of 'Big Daddy's' money to pay for whatever her sugar and spice heart desired. Even so, she never displayed luxurious taste. Amber loved dolls of all different classes. If she spotted a dirty doll in the mission window, she purchased it for a dollar, took it home, and cleaned it up good as knew. She collected Barbie, Strawberry Shortcake, Cabbage Patch Kids, Rainbow Brite, My Little Pony, and hand made dolls. And Ken was not the only cock in the hen house. Amber enjoyed 'boy' dolls just as much as 'girl' dolls. She bought GI Joe, Star Wars figures, Power Rangers, and Wrestling figures. All puppets and collectibles were accepted. She selected material- satin, lace, silk, polyester- for making doll dresses, paid the clerk, tipped him with a wink, and rushed outside, seeking Benjamin's opinion of her new toy. He did not nod, smile, or grant the slightest gesture. Yet Amber appeared to read his mind. She kissed him again as he opened the door for her.

While she got all gussied up in the beauty salon, Benjamin tended to the grocery shopping. You read it right- THE BEAUTY SALON! Ladies' faces lit up like Vegas every time Amber came in for a treatment. She deepened their laugh lines by telling silly stories of RJ's escapades. She talked about how he loved to watch cartoons and eat cereal. Whenever she discussed how concerned she was for his failing health in his old age, the ladies got misty. THEY WERE CRYING FOR RJ ROCKHOUSE! Hell had officially frozen over.

Honestly, town found it refreshing. Muddy Mountain scary stories had grown stale. Everybody was pleased to discover that all the fear had only been in their heads. Amber left the beauty salon with her strawberry strands radiating, clinging tightly to a new doll. Benjamin pulled to the curb. She slipped into the limo, and they made their way back up the mountain, where Big Daddy was strumming banjo, singing Old McDonald, and everyone had a merry, good ol' time.

That was the routine for nearly a decade. Some of the folks, who claimed to be present at Joe's pub the night Anthony waddled through the door like a poisoned possum, were still around. But they began to question the legitimacy of Anthony's story. Really, it was a ridiculous thing to believe that dogs would return from the grave and that rich men could eat coyotes alive.

Soon, everyone dismissed the tall tales all together and rumors of a new breed began to circulate. Gossip spread that

Amber was 'earning' Big Daddy's money. Hard to swallow, considering RJ was almost a century old, but stranger things have happened. Besides that, everyone has to talk about everyone else, and it is far more comfortable to say, 'RJ is taking that hot tot to bed,' than it is to say, 'RJ Rockhouse will drink your children's blood.'

So, everyone breathed easier for awhile. Then, one day, the convoy roared through town, pulling mobile homes. Bulldozers and dump trucks cleared paths through the mud. Contractors deciphered blueprints and building codes. Sugarland trailer park became a reality. Old Codger founded a community where the poor and misfortunate could start a new life, absolutely rent-free. Good things were happening at the hand of RJ Rockhouse, and everyone in town wondered why.

3.

In the beginning, there was nothing but muddy goo. Scores worth of tears, trickling from Muddy Mountain's peek, settled at the mouth and formed murky tundra, where no tree dare lay root and no flower dare spread seed. Briars cut thin crevasses throughout the soupy sludge. Leech infested moats, moss, and poison oak swallowed the land like quick sand. Not even the noblest knight would tarry through this valley. The mountain's mud sucked men down like Mother Nature's frown.

For three-quarters of a century, RJ capped Muddy Mountain like the sire of mire. He cared not for the slime. He cared not for the town.

"Let them eat shit," the king did permit.

Then, one morning, everything changed. RJ awoke to a brand new day. The window of his study opened like the eye of a newborn. RJ saw sunlight for the first time in ages. Naturally, he had seen the sun every day of his life, but not like today. The sun had always seemed to him like God's furious fist, reminding mankind with each passing day of the pathetic vulnerability of humanity; not today. Blue was blue and green was green; the way only unfiltered sunlight can brand it.

RJ viewed the world from his study window. He saw the deepest crease of every hollow. Town thickened just beyond Muddy Mountain's mouth. The people down there were building families, yet they were poor.

"Oh my God," he gurgled, "I'm either having an epiphany or a stroke."

Nine out of ten doctors would agree; RJ Rockhouse experienced an epiphany. The morning dawned on him with light so bright it was blinding. Adrenaline gushed through his varicose veins. Icicle limbs quivered. Dim eyes suddenly shined like lamps with fresh batteries.

"Them," he exclaimed, "They are the answer."

His inspiration was too virgin to be concrete. All he knew at that moment was that something had to be done with the muddy mess clogging the mountain's mouth like sewer sludge.

"What shall I do?" he wondered.

Perhaps he could erect a statue stretching high into the sky of Jesus, Zeus, or even Elvis. He quickly dismissed that notion. Something more mystical than the Sphinx and more seductive than Sodom needed to be built.

"What can I build that will draw the masses?" he questioned.

Suddenly, the answer echoed in his ears like holy-ghost whisper.

"A trailer park."

Everyone was surprised how quickly the project moved. In no time, the mud was chewed up by bulldozers and spit into dump trucks. The swampy delta had been ditched and dried. A coffee colored confection of topsoil, grass seed, fertilizer, and hay seasoned the vacant area.

On the eastern edge, men in hardhats constructed a playground, complete with monkey bars, jungle gyms, swing sets, seesaws, a basketball court, and a merry-go-round. On the western edge, lots were petitioned for homes. Water and sewer pipes tunneled through ditches like big arteries. Poles, as big as tree trunks, were set for electricity and telephone. The men in hardhats wove a wiry web throughout the area. The road received a fresh coating of asphalt. Finally, the cake was ready for its icing. A convoy of big rigs split the horizon like Alexander's army, pulling state of the art manufactured homes that were setting atop tiny wheels, which did not appear strong enough to support a bicycle frame, let alone a bulky trailer. Men in hardhats administered the finishing touches.

Thirteen homes now lined what had once been the most desolate grounds in southeast Kentucky. Muddy Mountain gave the scene a shadowy backdrop. Rockhouse's mansion crowned the mountain, watching everything like an oracle.

Word of Sugarland's opening quickly spread. My, oh my, did the people come. They oozed from every ghetto and hollow like swamp slime. Rickety rust buckets came sputtering in on wobbly wheels. Families spilled endlessly from each car like clowns in that classic circus trick. Children with dirty noses, loused hair, and crusty clothes immediately cut a path to the playground, unattended by their parents. Bearded men and toothless women spoke to each other from behind cheap cigarettes and silver coffee thermoses, halfway filled with java and halfway filled with... something else. The men tried, with no success, to tuck rat's nest hair beneath mesh caps. The women let their bleached nests fall freely in every direction for the world to marvel. Everyone sported similar outfits- faded flannel and dirty denim-like they had all borrowed clothes from the same uncle. They were a lowly breed, but RJ had given specific instructions that no one be turned away. Sugarland was founded on the first come first serve principle.

Rockhouse commissioned Franklin Bates to handle all paperwork that would be necessary for the tenants. Franklin was RJ's attorney from Lexington. RJ figured the best way to keep local politicians' fingers out of Sugarland's pie was to funnel all the paperwork through Franklin's office. He was happy to oblige. Rockhouse tipped handsomely. Franklin sat up a makeshift office in one of the trailers, and just like that, dreams became reality.

Rockhouse slumped at his study window trying to steady a pair of binoculars with freezing hands. He thought his heart would be warmed. Instead, he was overcome with deep sadness watching the crowd. The thirteen tenants were all families with fathers that were big enough to brut and bully their way past the others. When all was said and done, and the thirteen homes had been filled, RJ saw several single mothers gathering their children and walking away, struggling to hide tear filled eyes. Rockhouse could always spot a single mother, even from the top of a high mountain. Something about their frustrated faces and the way they tried to instill hope into their children, even when they had no hope themselves, touched RJ in a place he thought time had withered away.

"Thirteen is not enough."

Once again, here came the convoy, the men in hardhats, and Franklin Bates toting his briefcase. This time, RJ was pleased to see single mothers reaping the benefits of his benevolence. Thirty-six more families joined the community of thirteen. But wait... thirteen plus thirty-six equals forty-nine; how odd. In the beginning, there were not enough homes. Now, there was one too many. This would not have bothered RJ had it been three or four trailers. But just one empty house... the thought was unsettling. He gazed down upon it for hours. There was nothing wrong with the trailer. It looked exceedingly pretty sitting at the north end of the grounds like leader of the pack, with its beige siding and red trim shining in morning sunlight. It appeared so sad, watching, with dark windows, as the other homes enjoyed children's laughter. Families built memories inside all the other homes' slender walls. That one, red trimmed trailer sat like Cinderella at the north end of the grounds, weeping and wishing for an invitation to the ball. Rockhouse considered the empty home an omen.

"Something significant is going to come from that place."

He could not help but laugh and shake his head at such a strange sight.

"Surely," he sighed, "someone will show up."

4.

They could barely see for all the dust. Winter wind whipped southeast Kentucky hard and unforgiving. Dust was so thick Arthur needed the assistance of windshield wipers to see the road. He did not care; neither did Judith. God was not going to let them die; not today.

Judith gently rubbed Arthur's thigh. They were on their way to the land of dried tears. Sweet freedom flowed through Arthur's veins. His 1980 Chevy Malibu cut the highway like a streaking white bullet. Judith adjusted her glasses and reluctantly shuffled in the seat. Arthur smiled and patted her lovingly on the leg. Since the day she met him, he lit up her life like a neon marquis.

AND THEY LIVED HAPPILY EVER AFTER
STARRING JUDITH PAGE
Directed by: Arthur Addler

All they wanted, in the whole wide world, was to build a life together. This seemed impossible, until Arthur found a flier for Sugarland trailer park flipping in the winter breeze outside the grocery store where he worked. Rockhouse's generosity granted them hope of a new beginning. Now, they cruised along the dusty highway like a married couple, with bags full of their belongings cramping the trunk and back seat.

They approached Sugarland from the northern tip of the county, thus the dust. Most of the hills north of town had been leveled by surface mines, leaving flatland for miles around, all across the peripheral like a dessert.

Two miles outside of town the dust cloud cleared. Appalachia regained her beauty. Sharp peeked mountains poked the horizon like saw teeth. Town surrounded the foot of Muddy Mountain, shaping with the black creek bed. Judith flipped through radio stations, until she found Hank Williams Jr.

"A Country Boy Can Survive, hot damn," she hollered, waiting to sing along, "the preacher man says it's the end of time, and the Mississippi River, she's a going dry."

Arthur laughed and flinched against her sour key. Judith adjusted her glasses and squinted into December's low hanging sun.

"Speaking of rivers," she said, "you're gonna have to stop up here at the store. I'm out of tampons."

"You were just at the store this morning," he groaned, "have you gone through a whole box sense then?"

"If I bought tampons, I wouldn't have had enough money for my blueberry milkshake."

Arthur rolled his eyes.

"They serve those milkshakes in Styrofoam cups, don't they? Whittle yourself a tampon out of that."

Judith pulled her legs tight against her chest, sucked her face into a pucker, and rested her cheek against a knee.

"Come on, Arthur baby. Pwease. Pwease!"

Arthur pulled into the convenience store. His Malibu sputtered for a few seconds, even after he killed the ignition, reminding him that this stop had not been planned.

"You've done upset my baby," he whined.

"Arthur baby..."

"What?"

"Go in and get them for me."

"Why, Ju-Ju? You're big enough to have a period. You're big enough to buy plugs."

"I look like a scrub," she cried.

"Judith..."

"Please, Arthur; pretty please. This is my favorite song. I promise I'll make it up to you."

Arthur did the inevitable. He crawled out of the car and strutted into the store as proudly as a man buying tampons possibly could. Paying no mind to size, texture, or fragrance, he grabbed the first box of tampons he saw and made a B line for the cash register.

"You know, these aren't for me," he joked with the boy running the register, "they're for my hot girlfriend."

"Oh," the clerk sneered, motioning toward the window with his nose, "I thought they might have been for your daughter out there."

Arthur did not bother leaving a tip. He returned to the car half angered and half humored.

"There," he exclaimed, tossing the box onto Judith's lap, "you just wanted to see if you could make me do that, didn't you?"

"Ah, did it embarrass poor Arthur baby to have to buy tampons?"

"I got them didn't I?"

Judith rolled down the window and tunneled through her purse to find a cigarette.

"Why don't you roll up that window?" Arthur shivered.

"I just can't stand smoking in a car with the windows rolled up. I don't like having that smoke smell all over me."

"You're a smoker, angel. Whether you realize it or not, you smell like a smoker. Anyway, you don't need to smoke right now, so roll it up, okay, princess?"

Judith aborted the search for a cigarette and cranked the window closed. She nervously chewed a thumbnail.

"Baby, I'm scared."

"Seriously, Judith."

"I mean it. I'm scared. I've heard a lot of stories about RJ Rockhouse and that whacked out butler of his."

"Stories, exactly."

"You're not even a teensie-weensie bit scared?"

"No, Judith. I happen to be excited. How many months have we talked about getting our own place? This is it, honey. We can say 'to Hell' with your family and the whole damn world. If you ask me, RJ Rockhouse is a saint. Besides, Judith, you've got me with you. If a devil pops out of the closet, I'll just go upside his head."

Judith snickered but her shoulders continued to slump.

"I hear he's a vampire, Arthur. That's why he's lived so long."

"I don't think so," Arthur argued, "I think the reason he's lived so long is because he doesn't have a woman."

"Ha-Ha!"

"Think about it, Ju-Ju. We have maybe one murder a year in this county. If he's a vampire, he's not a very hungry one."

"He sends his butler out of town to find his victims."

"Well, there you go. You live in town, so there's nothing to worry about."

The road ran ruler straight out of town's rectum and into Sugarland. Judith's green eyes glittered as she soaked up the image of her brand new aluminum community. She wagged her tail like a happy puppy, counting the trailers and wondering which one was HERS. Children gathered on the playground, spinning on the merry-go-round, rising and falling on the seesaw, and scaling the monkey bars' rungs with synchronized motions like baby machines.

"Over there," said Arthur, squinting into the sunlight, "in the first driveway over yonder, that's a black Lincoln isn't it?"

"I guess so."

"That's the car we're looking for. That must be our place right there?"

They pulled into lot #1. Franklin Bates met them immediately like a man with a million places to be. He looked like a lawyer- brown coat, white shirt, brown tie, black briefcase; brown hair with random patches of gray surrounding a perfectly oval chrome dome; beady brown eyes behind thick glasses; thin brown moustache; brisk stride; interrogating expression.

"Arthur Addler?" he questioned.

"Yep, that's me."

"I am Franklin Bates, Mr. Rockhouse's attorney. This is it, your new place. Inside, on the bar, are a few papers for you to fill out. Once you have all the information we need, you can mail the papers to my office. The keys are also on the bar. Is this lady here Miss Page?"

"Yeah, she'll be living here, too."

"Yes, Mr. Rockhouse has left a special gift for her inside. It's a book. I must be going," said Bates, already halfway in his car, "everything is working properly inside the home. If you have any questions, feel free to phone my office."

No sooner than he spat out the words, Franklin Bates' car disappeared in a cloud of dust.

"Friendly fella ain't he?" Arthur chuckled.

"He said Mr. Rockhouse left me a book," Judith gasped, "I don't like that. I don't like that at all."

"Relax, Judith. It'll do you some good to read."

The inside of the home smelled brand new. Blue carpet was firm and un-matted. Paneling glistened on the walls. The linoleum and appliances were unstained. On top the oak colored bar, acting as a partition between the kitchen and living room, sat the papers for Arthur to fill out and a book with a card on top that simply read, "For Judith". Judith picked up the book and examined it wryly.

"Women Who Run With Wolves, by Clarissa Pinkola Estés,"

Judith read, slowly sounding out the author's name, "what kind of freakazoid gift is this?"

"Women Who Run With Wolves," Arthur smirked, "old Rockhouse must not know you very well. You don't read or run."

"Shut up, Arthur," Judith whined, punching him jokingly on the shoulder, "I can't wait to get started decorating this place. Let's hurry up and get our stuff unpacked."

5.

Midnight donned an illustrious hue of indigo. Arthur was at peace with God. Beer-bottle sweat slipped over his fingers and gathered into puddle on his bare chest. He lounged freely on the sofa, wearing nothing but blue boxers. The television was on. Songs downloaded on the computer. And Judith- good God-burned like a kerosene candle. She fluttered freely through the home, folding clothes and cozying all their belongings in various corners of her new cocoon. Caramel hair smoothed into a loose ponytail, wagging at her shoulders. Arthur's white t-shirt made the perfect nightgown, as far as he was concerned.

Judith positioned everything precisely throughout the home, trying her best to 'woman' the place up. Arthur did not mind. He stretched on the sofa, ninety percent naked, with a cold beer and free television. What more could a man ask for?

"Give me one of those beers," Judith demanded, wiping sweat from her glasses on Arthur's shirt.

"You're underage, young'un," Arthur joked, "you won't be legal drinking age for another three years."

"Tell it to the judge, Mr. Statutory."

Arthur had no retort. He slow poked to the refrigerator and fetched Judith a cold one.

"If you're gonna drink my beer, you're gonna fold my clothes. You know that don't you?"

"I am folding your clothes, doofus. I have everything arranged in the closet. Your clothes are hanging to the far right. Mine are hanging in the middle and on the left. My shoes are in boxes stacked on the floor. My jewelry and makeup are in boxes on the shelf. Your underwear and socks are in the top dresser drawer. The rest of the drawers are full of my stuff."

"Hey now," Arthur burped, "make sure you don't cheat yourself."

"I can't help it, baby. You don't have many clothes."

"Isn't that the way it goes between a man and a woman? You

have lots of clothes. I don't have many. But you still wear one of my shirts as a nightgown."

"I don't hear you complaining, prick."

He hugged her from behind. His arms were firm from the many cases of laundry detergent and spaghetti sauce he had stocked. She melted in his hands.

Arthur returned to the sofa. Judith returned to her bags and boxes. She picked through panties, stacking them in color-coordinated piles, until she uncovered Rockhouse's book.

"Women Who Run With Wolves," she repeated. A cold shiver brushed her shoulders, "God, that man freaks me out."

"Jesus, Judith! That old man ain't no monster. It's all just a game he plays. He's like them goth girls you meet in high school. He likes to be evil because he thinks it makes him cool."

"Yeah, well, I'll tell you something, Arthur. Some of them goth girls really will drink your blood. And I'll tell you something else. That old creep scares me. I don't like him. He might catch me here all by myself and try to eat me."

"I can't say I blame him there."

"Eww! I'm just a little freaked out. I don't like the thought of having to stay here alone at night."

"Would it make you feel any better if I bought some garlic? I can whittle us some wooden stakes. Jesus! I can't believe I'm having this conversation. The old dude just gave you a house."

"And that doesn't seem strange to you?"

"No. He's a rich, old, lonely man just trying to get things even with God so he can make it into Heaven."

"Shut up, Arthur! You're scared of meeting him, too. I can see it all over you every time a vehicle goes by. You get all quiet and fidgety. You're scared too, so don't talk to me like I'm a little kid."

Arthur could sense the time for teasing had come to an end. He sat his beer down and stood to comfort her.

"I'm sorry," he conceded, hugging her again, "you're right. He does freak me out a little. And I understand why you are. But he's not a vampire, honey baby. A weird, old pervert maybe, but not a vampire. You know that. You also know that there ain't a damn thing gonna hurt you while I'm with you. The store is just five minutes from here. You can call me anytime you get scared, and I'll be right to your side."

She snuggled his embrace and buried glasses in his chest.

"I love you, Arthur."

"I love you, Judith. You know, if I thought for one second there was anything here that was gonna hurt you, I'd rip you up, carry you off, and we would- someway, somehow- find someplace."

She pulled his head to her lips and kissed him for a long, long while.

"I know you're right, Arthur. But you've got to do one thing for me. You've got to teach me how to shoot a gun."

"No way," he grinned.

"Why not?"

"Because I'm afraid, if I taught you to use a gun, you'd shoot somebody."

Arthur teed a cigarette between Judith's lips and sat it ablaze, while wiping sweat from her glasses. Her silence seemed uneasy.

"Arthur baby?"

"Yes, Ju-Ju."

"Will you fix me a milkshake?"

"Absolutely, Judith. I will fix you a milkshake in our new blender. Then you can drink it on our new couch while watching our new TV."

Arthur had no need for kitchen lights. Midnight cast a glow that brightened everything blue like a lighted globe. He spooned vanilla ice cream and blueberries into the blender, added milk accordingly, sang a happy song, then returned to the living room, handed Judith the shake, and wedged beside her on the sofa. They watched the evening news like a grownup couple. Meteorologists and anchors bickered over Arctic cold fronts, Gulf Stream currents, and barometric pressures. Everyone agreed on only one variable. Blizzard clouds would soon canopy Kentucky skies.

Second Quarter
The Great Fall
1.

RJ remembered a time when eastern Kentucky was one forest. Prickly pines, broad oaks, sap sticky maples, and tall poplars merrily joined branches in a chain of wilderness expanding from the Ohio River to the Cumberland Gap, as far as the eye could see.

His early childhood memories consisted mostly of barefoot travels across the forest's tender moss carpeting and through cool creek waters so thick with minnows and crawdads you could scoop them up in your hand without ever looking down.

Beaver, deer, bears, and wildcats roamed freely and carelessly through the woods like people at a Sunday morning marketplace. Nature produced enough of everything for everything. Kentucky was a vast cornucopia filled with all the fruit, meat, milk, and water anything would need for generations to come. Not many generations passed before RJ noticed the change. Kentucky's one great forest segmented into many smaller forests. Somehow, RJ felt he was to blame.

Many years before RJ's birth, most of America experienced an industrial revolution. Assembly lines and new innovations in transportation magically changed Jules Verne's fiction into science, seemingly overnight. Factories popped up in all the urban areas. Suddenly, life had a fast lane.

Rumors spread that Yankees were building Babble sized towers in New York City. The country's pulse quickened- except for Kentucky. Kentucky proudly preserved her heritage. There were no skyscrapers threatening to poke God in the eye; no subway system ripping holes through Mother Nature's gut. Kentuckians still considered the fowl of the air and the lily of the field. Perhaps this sentiment could have lasted forever had Kentucky continued to belong to Kentuckians. Like Eve, Kentucky's great fall came at the hands of deception, and Eden was forever lost.

Deep within Kentucky's virgin loins was a mineral the country needed to keep its pulse rapid. Beneath those prickly pines and tender moss lay tons upon tons of precious coal. Shrewd businessmen like JP Morgan and Thomas Rockhouse realized early the financial opportunity coal could provide. Wall Street wolves slipped on sheep's clothing and came to huff, puff, and blow down Kentucky's straw house.

Articulate lawyers visited poor, hick farmers, flashing fancy words like *stock dividend, interest rate percentage, and* MINERAL RIGHTS. Soon, nearly all of Kentucky had been cheated out of its land.

Thomas Rockhouse, father of RJ, built a black gold empire on the backs of the impoverished. After Thomas died, his son inherited the dirty curse. RJ seemed poised to make right what his father wronged, until Lola died. After that, RJ no longer cared for people, but he did hold on to his reverent respect for the mountains.

He spent a great deal of time walking paths that weaved through the forest for miles and miles behind his mansion. Squirrels scurried toward the click of his cane and chirped gratefully, as he fed them crumbs from his pockets. RJ rested in the shade of the very same trees he climbed as a lad. Now, most of those trees were crook backed and decaying the same as he. Occasionally, if he had the energy, RJ toted his cane-pole to the river bank to waste the day fishing for bluegill. When he was a young man, catching bluegill was as simple as catching fireflies. Now, however, the river had depleted like his veins, and a man could sit silently for hours without ever getting a bite.

It did not please him to watch the mountain wither, but it did give him something to which he could relate. Sometimes, he spoke to the trees like they were old, familiar friends that understood perfectly every feeling festering in his heart. And he swore that no matter how feeble he grew, his walks through the mountain would not cease until the day his ashes were scattered there.

That is how RJ discovered Amber on that gentle spring day when he was eighty-nine years old. By all means, he should not have been walking in the woods that morning. After all, he was eighty-nine. He could sense the weakness of his heart, and his fragile joints ached with a nearly crippling pain. But RJ had a bond with the mountain, and it was a bond he would not break even if it killed him.

A long, rock cliff, stretching approximately fifty feet tall, capped the western edge of Muddy Mountain. It had been quite some time since RJ visited that side of the estate. As fate would have it, the rocky cliff was his destination that morning.

Right away, he spotted the body lying lifelessly in the sand. Although he knew what he saw, RJ simply could not convince himself to believe that is was the broken body of a girl.

He hurried to her side, as quickly as an eighty-nine year old man can, and kneeled beside her. She was a beautiful young lady, maybe fifteen or sixteen years old. Her lily skin had barely a scratch on it, but her chest was not moving and blood oozed from her mouth. RJ deduced that the girl must have been walking in the woods and somehow carelessly tumbled from atop the rock cliff. He fancied her for dead.

"Young lady," he muttered, "the best thing you can hope for now is that the buzzards come to relieve you of your misery."

RJ returned to the mansion with no great haste and fetched Benjamin. Benjamin ventured into the forest on an ATV, retrieved the broken girl, and brought her home. Six months later it was unapparent that Amber had ever been so close to death. She skipped without stagger and chirped without stutter. Physically, she was as fit as she had ever been, but her rehabilitation did not come without a cost. When Amber awoke from her great fall, she had no memory of anything. She did not know her name nor could she remember the faces or names of any family. Why she ventured in the woods remained a mystery. Her mind was full of questions that had no answers. Days went by; then weeks; then months and still not even the slightest recollection surfaced. Even more perplexing was the fact that no one ever came looking for Amber. There were no bulletins announcing her disappearance. In all the times she had been into town not one person ever claimed to recognize her. It was almost as if she had fallen from Heaven.

After awhile, RJ figured it would be safe to claim her as his own. So, he gave her a name, "Amber". He gave her a home and dressed her up like a doll. Ten years passed, and eventually town grew to adore Amber. Most of the time, she seemed happy. But Amber was different than everyone else, and it was not just the amnesia. Observing Amber made it obvious that something inside of her was not right. Some folks could argue that she had received slight brain damage as a result of her great fall. But regardless of the reasoning, Amber was strange, and what bothered her most was the fact that she knew the true reason why.

2.

November 29,
Baby sister Judith,
On this darkest of nights, when the stars harden like scabs and the moon's lid closes to a sleepy sliver, I pray only one prayer on my own behalf. I pray that God guides this letter safely into your hands, and that He inspires you to respond with the warmest of words.

It has been two years since last we spoke. I think of you daily, and I love you now more than ever. Since our last correspondence, I have entered my graduate studies. As soon as this mission is finished (God willing) I will have my master's degree in Christian theology, and I will finally be ready to minister my own church.

This prize does not come without a price. My missionary obligations have landed me in The Badlands of China. Dearest sister, I cannot properly pen the dark oppression that looms across this land like Satan's storm cloud. Everything is different here. *The Emperor's* image hangs on every building, and those, who refuse to bow down, are subsequent to beheading, just like what John prophesied in 'The Book of Revelations'. Christianity is considered treason. Those caught spreading Christianity, be they Chinese, American, or Martian are sentenced to death and their memories erased. My mind is vexed by constant paranoia. But my faith is strong, and the people here have proven to be very helpful.

My advisor secured me sanctuary in the Lu house. The Lu's are kind, Christian folk. In many respects, they are responsible for saving my life. They organize the church services, which take place Tuesday nights in the back of a bar/chapel. Whenever the Red Army becomes suspicious and makes their rounds, the Lu's hide me in a chest that is frighteningly familiar to a coffin. Red Soldiers swarm the tiny hut. Their boot heals click back and forth along my horizontal body. Their constant queries unearth nothing but devout praise for the almighty emperor, yet they are suspicious.

Enough about the incompetent crimsons, I have survived their impromptu raids for eight months. I have the utmost faith that I can weather them for four more.

Two concerns darken me like shadows. If I fail in my graduate mission, one of these two tribulations will certainly carry the blame. I have grown grievously homesick, little sister. Nothing in these Badlands is familiar to home. The villages are cramped, and the huts are crudely constructed. Very few people speak English. Even their musical instruments seem to bleed a foreign language. Without the assistance of the Lu's, I would be totally lost, and this colossal country would devour me. Most of my time is spent in the dark either hiding or resting with nothing but my faith in God and thoughts of home to light the dreary path.

Four months is all I have remaining. I have no doubt that these will be the longest four months of my life. I am a soldier stationed in a far away, strange land, fighting a war with words instead of bullets. A reply from you will revive my lonely spirit. Please, Judith, I beg of you. Write me a letter. Even if it is only to say, 'Hello, brother, I love you and miss you.' You have always been a fervent supporter of my ambitions. I need your blessings now more than ever.

Homesickness, however, is not my chief concern. I have not slept in two days. My temperament has grown paranoid. Even now, my hands are trembling so violently I can hardly hold pen to paper. I experienced things in this house that have changed me so drastically I fear that I may never again know the pleasure of a serene soul. I do not expect you to believe what I am about to tell you. In fact, I would rather you not believe my story. But I must share this tale with someone. The longer I keep my fears bottled up, the more they fester.

The home consists of four persons (minus me). There is a mother, a father, and a teenage son. These three have opened their home to me with grace and compassion. All three speak English, and they have served as my tongue for the better part of a year. I also realize that they stake their existence for me on a daily basis. There is no doubt in my mind that these three would lay down their lives for my ministry.

However, they are not the central focus of my story. Perhaps they should be. If so, I pray God will forgive me. The fourth member of the family is the one that weighs heaviest on my mind.

Everyone calls him Max. I do not know if this is his given name, but it is the only name I have ever heard the family call him. Max is an elderly man. He has no tongue. The only sounds he can muster are gurgles, grunts, and laughs. Max's eyes are endless ebony pits. What I mean to say is that he has no eyeballs. His eyelids sag over empty craters. There is no question in my mind should one dare to venture close enough, one could see through Max's sockets all the way to his brain. Where his ears should be, there is nothing but pruned flesh, covering shriveling shafts like curtains.

The Lu's claim that Max was once a great minister for Christ and that he lost his tongue, eyes, and ears to the imperial army. I do not wish to falsely accuse my gracious hosts, but I cannot help feeling that they are hiding something. Maybe I am jumping to conclusions, but Max does not seem like a righteous martyr to me.

The family keeps him shelved in the attic. Throughout sunlight hours, he rests on a scarlet rug with his legs crossed meditation style and his open palms stretched forward, as if he is awaiting a great sacrifice. Most times he is content and silent. The family takes turns spooning him mush.

I have visited him in the attic only a handful of times. The sight of the old man is more than I can tolerate. He sits still on a red rug in the center of a dusty, plywood floor. As a matter of fact, he sits so still, one could easily mistake him for a sculpture. His hands stretch forward. Long, baize nails crown each fingertip. A black robe swallows him like a skeleton dressed in a burial shroud. Max's head is bald, with the exception of one silver dollar sized patch of white hair sprouting from the rear concave of his scalp and spiraling to the floor. His face remains angled to the side. Hallow eye-pits seem to suck all light from the room. Max greets his visitors with a toothless smile like a skull captured in the midst of ecstasy. Flies swarm the infected flaps where his ears should be.

Three times a day, one of the Lu's climbs the stairs to the attic. They spoon feed Max mush. He gurgles excitedly. Brown bubbles burst on his lips, and sticky sludge collects on his chin. The whole while, Max remains perfectly still. For quite sometime, I was able to lock the old man away in the attic of my mind, until the night he came creeping downstairs.

The Lu's sleep in dens at the far corner of the house. Their quarters are separated from the attic stairs by many curving corridors and several rooms, such as the kitchen and the study. I, however, am not so fortunate. I bunk in a small room at the foot of Max's staircase. His gurgles and snores cut my sleep like shards of glass. One night, just a few weeks ago, I awoke to the sound of feet scampering through the hall outside my quarters. The sound of heavy, trotting feet echoed in the hall, entered my bedroom, shuffled to the head of my bed, exited again to the hall, climbed a few of Max's stairs, and then continued the trek over and over again. All the while I watched the hall with wide, curious eyes. Not once did I spot an image that could correspond with the fervent patter of feet.

I was calm at first. I did not allow my fears to overcome me. This escapade continued for perhaps half an hour. Then the entity scurried into my room and halted its haste at the head of my bed. All was silent for a minute or so.

I stared straight ahead through the air where the being stood. I could see nothing out of the ordinary. But the atmosphere tattled on my paranormal imposter. The temperature turned frigid. An eerie aura consumed the room. So help me, Savior, I heard giggling, soft yet macabre, directly adjacent to my ear. My heart began to hurt, and quietly I prayed.

The spirit exited my room with hurried steps and climbed the attic stairs. Once again, all was silent for a moment. Then Max let out a moan that was sad and deep like the plea of a man too frightened to scream.

What I next witnessed challenged my faith more than any other experience I have ever known. Fear's claws cut gashes through my gut. The haunted, cold air rendered my tongue bitterly arid.

There was a curious creaking of the ceiling-boards above my bed. The creak slithered like a snake across the attic floor to the summit of the stairs. Max's robe spilled down the stairs like a shadow, and the old man descended. His face remained cocked to the side. Open palms held steady like antenna at the ends of erect arms. Max tip toed into my room and stopped with perfect precision at the head of my bed. His hideous face turned down toward me, as if he actually had eyes. The tiny nub of severed tongue in the back of his toothless pit of a mouth flapped with a wet, clicking sound. Yellow palms roamed my body, loosely inquisitive like the hands of a physician. I did not know what to do; so, I prayed. I prayed with the intensity of Daniel, locked in the lions' den. I prayed as he frisked my very soul. This continued for maybe fifteen minutes. Then Max tip toed out of my room and returned to his perch in the cocoon of the attic.

Now, I lie quaking in my quarters, praying for courage and sleep. But do not fear for me, sister. I am strong, and I have finally reached the last leg of my tribulation. Please write to me. Send your correspondence to the enclosed address. I love you, and I look forward to having dinner with you four months from now, unless you're the one doing the cooking... Sorry, I had to end my letter with humor.

Your loving brother,

Seth

"Oh my God," Judith gasped, "I'm worried about my brother. What's going on, Arthur?"

"I don't know," Arthur answered.

Judith took a seat at the kitchen table without bothering to turn on the light. She lit a cigarette and let the smoke plume all around her in the beam of streetlight spilling through the window.

"Seth is talking crazy," she continued, "I think he might be losing his mind."

"He's probably experiencing culture shock," Arthur concluded, slipping a sweat shirt over his shoulders in the living room and checking his pack of cigarettes to see if he had enough to do him until he got to work.

"What do you mean?"

"Judith, he's in the middle of China. Things are different there than they are here. The Chinese culture is one of the oldest in the world. He's probably just freaked out. God knows I would be. Anyway, if I were you, I'd be more concerned with the red army than that creepy geezer living in the attic."

Instantly, he knew he said the wrong thing. Judith's eyes swelled with tears.

"No, I didn't mean that the way it sounded. Seriously, Judith, he's going to be fine. He just has four more months. What you need to concentrate on is writing him a cheery letter that will lift his spirits. And try to think about what a good time you all are going to have when he returns home."

"Yeah, I guess you're right," she sighed, "but I have no idea what to say to him."

"Your brother seems very articulate."

"What do you mean?"

"I can tell from his letter that he is educated. He's well spoken."

"Yeah, bubby always was good with books. He spent some time in juvie when he was a kid. The rest of the times he shuffled back and forth between foster homes. Bubby never did have much for entertainment, so he read a lot."

"Well, there's nothing wrong with an education," Arthur said, moving to the kitchen and rummaging through the cabinets for something to pack in his lunch bucket, "God knows I wish I had an education right about now."

Judith sucked her cigarette all the way down to the cotton.

"Bubby is the only one in my biological family that ever bothered to keep in touch with me. Brenda had seven kids by seven different men. Can you believe that? What a whore. Seth is the only boy. I am his only baby sister. The older sisters have all treated him like crap. Seth told me one time that every foster home he ever went to had at least one Bible. Reading the Bible is what turned him onto Jesus. He told me once that he's glad he had to go through all them abusive foster homes because if he hadn't, he may have never met God. He always was funny like that."

"That's a great philosophy," Arthur assured, dumping a couple of microwave pizzas into his lunch bucket, "he's going to be fine, Judith. God will protect him. You cheer up now. Seth needs you in good spirits."

Judith pushed the ashtray away and smiled tenderly at Arthur.

"I don't like you moping around here like this," Arthur babied, "Are you gonna be okay while I'm gone to work?"

"Yeah, I'll be fine," she smiled, "I made a new friend."

"Here in the trailer park?"

"Yeah, her name is Shirley. She lives on lot six. She's pretty cool."

"Well, that's great," he answered, surprised, "does she live by herself?"

"She has a kid, Brandon. He's four years old. She doesn't have anything to do of the night either, so she asked me to come hang out."

"Cool. I'm glad you have a friend."

Judith hooked her wrist across Arthur's forearm and sensually stroked his leathery skin. They sat in silence, dreading the oncoming storm.

"When I get to work, I'm going to buy up some cigarettes and a few groceries for us. The weatherman says we got some bad stuff heading in our direction tonight."

Judith snuggled her caramel head in his hard chest.

"Oh, baby, are you going to be okay driving in that madness?"

"The Malibu goes pretty descent in the snow. But if we get a blizzard like they're predicting, I'll have to leave it parked at the store and bum a ride off one of the guys at work with a four-wheel drive. But I'll be fine."

With the remaining moments before Arthur's departure, they rested on the sofa, stationary and serene. Arthur cradled Judith like an oversized baby, occasionally flicking a stray hair from the rim of her glasses and chicken pecking her lovingly on the forehead. The television and radio were off. The only light burning came from a sixty watt halogen in the hall. The scene was lifeless yet loving, with all the peaceful content of slumber. Fearing that sleep might overcome them, Judith arose and strolled to the window, pulling her robe snug. Peering into the night, she solemnly sighed.

"It's starting to snow."

Trickling flurries forewarned the storm. Shortly thereafter wind burst into howl. Over a foot of snow accumulated in an instant. Power lines plummeted, and within the snap of a finger, town turned black and white simultaneously. Winds were not the fiercest in recorded history. The precipitation broke no record. Yet that year's blizzard would undeniably go down as the worst town had ever known.

3.

Amber spent a lot of time outside. In the spring, she planted flowerbeds. One year, the entire eastern edge of Rockhouse manor served as a vegetable garden. Benjamin learned that he had been relieved of lawn mowing duties, at the cost of a throbbing pinky. Little Miss Rockhouse didn't hesitate to swat the knuckles of anyone touching her lawnmower. Other projects she thought were necessary, such as painting the house or cleaning the windows, received attention regularly.

Amber did not pass time outside because she enjoyed doing chores. In fact, most of her outdoor projects remained unfinished. Parts of the mansion were painted green. Other sections gleamed pink or orange or whatever the color of the month might be. Her flowerbeds and garden fell to the fate of weeds and insects. Truthfully, Amber often escaped outside because she suffered from claustrophobia. The condition never festered into mania. However, at times it did cause her to smother and have anxiety attacks.

She found the claustrophobia ironic, considering that her home was larger than any in the southeastern section of Kentucky. Yet, as spacious as it was, even the mansion seemed to close in on her at times.

Every now and then, she mentioned her claustrophobia to RJ. But he never devoted attention to it. As for Benjamin, she was lucky to get a grunt from him, if any response at all. So, Uncle Ben remained oblivious to personal matters like diarrhea, yeast infections, and claustrophobia, although she wanted to discuss her fear with him sometimes, in the car. Cars were horrible for Amber. On rides into town, she kept calm by preoccupying her mind with thoughts of dolls and possible ways to gussy them up. This method worked. Still, she knew that more than an hour in the car would likely lead to a freak out session.

Whenever anxiety attacks occurred in the mansion, Amber

attempted to regain composure by spending a little time outside. It did not matter if the sky brought forth sunshine, rain, or even a second Ice-Age. The very day after town's first blizzard in fourteen years, Amber trudged through the backyard in drifts up to her knees. Snow seemed less dense in the forest. So, she took a walk down RJ's wilderness trail, all the way to the rock cliffs, where she had her great fall.

At first, the crisp air and sugar coated scenery inspired peaceful emotion. But eventually, her spirits sank. Winter can be a depressing season in Appalachia. What the cold doesn't kill, it makes miserable. Death loomed with every turn- whether it be a lonely tree, fallen and rotting on the forest floor, a once bubbling brook, now frozen brittle and still, or an actual living, breathing creature, lost to winter's cruel desolation. It was a sight such as this that stopped Amber in her tracks and reduced her to tears. She kneeled in a spot along the path where snow wasn't as thick, tracing the outline of a pit bull with tear filled eyes. Amber knew of pit bulls, although she had never seen one. Why this domestic creature lay dead, miles into the wild remained a mystery. Folks in town branded pit bulls as villains, but nothing is more villainous than death. The harshest antagonist becomes a meek victim, once "Old Grim" enters the scene.

"What happened to you?" she whispered, "What have you done?"

Amber returned home, depressed, with mortality heavy on her mind. Death is the most claustrophobic of circumstances. Every day the walls close in tighter. No matter how fast or far you run, cruel fate is only one step behind. It might take ten seconds or one hundred years, but eventually doom taps you on the shoulder. There is no need to plead, bargain, or cry. A cold, cramped coffin is all that remains.

Amber's thoughts served no purpose other than torment. She didn't want to think about death or her walk through the wilderness anymore. So, she crawled into bed and slept until the following morning.

The next day went better. She woke up with an epiphany. Although doom is inevitable for a person's body, the human spirit can live on earth forever. Spirits transcend death through creation. Some people create children and become parents. After the parents are dead, the children continue living and become parents themselves. Thus, the establishment of a new generation preserves the spirits of those who came before. Other people use works of art, careers, or community service as a means of creativity. Regardless of the method, creation is the key to a spirit's eternal life. This revelation soothed Amber's depression and sparked an artistic mood.

She needed to channel her muse, so Amber once again took a walk down RJ's wilderness trail, this time unimpeded by the mountain's desolation. She pondered what to create. Something with snow seemed appropriate. After all, snow represents winter and winter represents dying. So, to bring snow to life would be like making a mockery of death. Suddenly, she found inspiration.

Near the entrance of RJ's wilderness trail, at the far edge of the backyard, Amber began building a snowman. No specific details immediately came to mind, other than, "This snowman has to be BIG!"

She constructed a base spanning large enough to cover her desired area. Once the torso and head were sculpted, she stood atop concrete blocks to place them in position. Because the snow was thick and firm, this process took only a matter of minutes. Amber stepped back and marveled at the mountain of a snowman, estimating him to tower about eight feet tall.

"Oh baby," she cheered, "ain't you a big boy? Now it's time to add a little pizzazz."

The mansion's attic was nothing short of a scene straight out of a nightmare. It had been used for storage since day one, and a house can accumulate a lot of junk over the course of a century. Walking through the attic was like trying to dance wearing rubber stilts. Every step presented the possibility of lacerating a toe on shards of glass, hidden beneath debris. In the winter there are no spiders. However, rats do not take winters off. Occasionally, one could be heard squeaking in the corner. Moldy smelling boxes full of old, useless crap cluttered the floor so badly, in some places it was impossible to move forward without first moving backwards and to the side.

There was a time when Amber visited the attic frequently to snoop through RJ's belongings and possibly scavenge something to use with her dolls. It had been almost three years since her last scavenger hunt. She never really liked going up there. Every visit was the same. For about ten minutes, curiosity intrigued her, and she got a big kick out of all the goofy looking old stuff cramped into countless cardboard boxes. But after ten minutes, the uneasy feeling of something watching her triggered claustrophobic paranoia, which led to a panicked dash out of the attic, sending piles of ancient junk flying in every direction.

There was no uneasy feeling today. Amber knew what she wanted and exactly where to find it. A metal trunk sat a few feet inside the attic's entrance, containing some of RJ's ritzy stuff from back in the day, such as a top hat, cane, and cufflinks. Amber dug through the trunk until she found the top hat. It once glistened black, erect, shiny, and new. Now a dull hue of grayish brown revealed the relic's neglect. Its posture slumped and its brittle brim sagged shamefully. Sitting unattended in the attic for seventy-five years did more wear and tear to the hat than one hundred years of steady adorning could. As Amber continued fishing, she wondered if RJ had been a snowman at one time. He seemed to have all the appropriate dressings- a sophisticated looking tobacco pipe, a long, tattered, black scarf, dark spectacles, and a large black button for the nose. Once the accessories were selected, she hurried back to the snowman before any creepy spirit thingies had the chance to spook her.

"Now, let's give that buff body a handsome face," she commanded, climbing the concrete blocks, while carrying Frosty's facial features.

Finally the masterpiece stood complete, atop a mountain too high for anyone to see, in the backyard of a freaky mansion that nobody visited. Yet Amber felt great pride in a humored sort of way. If her snowman were a finger painting, she would certainly hang him on the refrigerator.

From down in the hollow, a vehicle came chugging through snow like a mule. At first, Amber assumed it to be a plow or salt truck. The highway department began working on roads before the blizzard even began. After precipitation fell, a non stop fleet of pickup trucks and heavy equipment labored to carve paths through winter's icy wrath. They always cleared the road up Muddy Mountain, despite a state law prohibiting government equipment from maintaining private property. Even though local politicians never got a dime of RJ's money, they knew he had it, and they figured keeping him happy was worth while, as long as it meant he would not lend campaign contributions to their opponents. So, on occasion, the grumble of heavy duty engines echoed from the hollows.

This time, however, the vehicle ascending Muddy Mountain sounded less confident than the roaring plows, which interrupted Amber's sleep that morning. Curiosity overcame creativity. So, she abandoned her snowman and hurried toward the front yard to spy on Muddy Mountain's determined traveler.

A four-wheel drive diesel pickup, that sounded like it needed four more wheels to do the job, crawled its way up the road, spinning here and sputtering there. Its trek was slow, but its fervor diligent. Amber curiously followed every inch the determined truck labored to ascend Muddy Mountain's snowy slope.

Eventually, the stubborn pickup made it to the summit. Chains wrapped the tires and sandbags filled the bed, giving much needed traction against slippery conditions. Amber was surprised to see that the driver was Sheriff Kurt Bochester. She recognized him from the TV news. He wore one of those brown derbies with a star on the front like you see cops wear in movies. A thick, brown, leather jacket shaped with his broad shoulders. From his left breast, a badge gleamed in the snow's bright glare. He did not speak a word until he was close enough for Amber to touch him. The sheriff looked her over with innocent fascination.

"Mornin', ma'am. I thought roses wilted in the snow."

Amber cackled nervously. That was the last thing she expected him to say.

"You're just being silly, sheriff."

"Forgive me, ma'am," he chuckled, extending a strong, steady hand for her to shake, "I didn't mean to be rude. Have we met?"

"No," Amber blushed, "but I know who you are, Sheriff Bochester."

"It's an honor to make your acquaintance, ma'am."

"My name's Amber, sheriff," she giggled, enjoying his firm yet gentle grip, "very nice to meet you, unless I'm in trouble. I'm not in trouble am I?"

"No, no. If you are, I ain't found out about it yet. I'm just lookin' for a fella. I want to give you some details about him incase you see him, and I figure if we ain't found him by the time this snow melts, we might comb through some of the woods back here on Mr. Rockhouse's property."

The sheriff was ruggedly handsome. He appeared to be in his late thirties. Bushy eyebrows, the color of grain, sprouted from atop blue eyes and nearly kissed the brim of his derby. A well-trimmed moustache covered his top lip. The sheriff was not a brute, yet he gave the appearance of a man stout enough to bend steel. Amber's smiling eyes wandered over him.

"Is there a thief or some kind of crazy killer hiding out on our mountain?"

"No, it's nothing like that," he laughed pleasantly, "it's my brother. He's run off again. He does this every so often. But I'm a little worried about him this time. He's been gone four days, and now we've got all this snow."

"What makes you think he's up here?"

"Oh, ma'am, I don't think he'd come here to the house. The last place anybody saw him was back on the old Blue Star mine site. About the only way he could've gone into the woods would be to cross the creek and head up the other side of this mountain. Of course, I don't think that's what happened. If I's worried about it, I'd be searching the hills and dragging the river right now. I figure he's snowed in with a girl somewhere. But if he ain't showed up after this snow melts, we'll need to get a search party together. And we'll probably look back in this mountain."

"What makes him wanna run off like that?"

"Ah, he's a wild boy who likes wild women. You know what wild women will do to a man. But he'll probably turn up pretty soon, when he's out of money. Just incase, I want you to keep your eyes and ears open."

"Sure."

"His name's EJ. He's twenty-six years old, stands about 5'10". He has jet-black hair, fair skin, and blue eyes. There are tattoos all over him. He's got his initials 'EJ' tattooed on the back of his left hand."

This exchange totally caught Kurt off guard. All morning he dreaded driving to Rockhouse's mansion. Even the sheriff flushed with goose bumps at the mention of RJ's name. Kurt had no idea what to expect. He figured he would be all tense and squirmy talking to RJ, like a little girl who opens the shower curtain to find a big hairy spider. During the drive up Muddy Mountain, he prepped himself to maintain a stern, matter of fact demeanor. Yet there he stood, chatting with one of the cutest women he had ever seen. This, he had not prepared for. Kurt knew of Amber's existence, and he heard that she was good looking, but he never paid those rumors any mind. To him, Muddy Mountain was nothing more than the lair of an old zombie/werewolf/vampire/cannibal.

Amber's strawberry curls popped against winter's white backdrop. Her pink sweater and blue jeans clung tightly to every firm curve. Wild passion gleamed in her eyes, yet her actions were timid and shy. Kurt didn't know what to think. She seemed like a woman who would cuss and pray at the same time. One thing was for sure, Amber Rockhouse gave a fascinating first impression.

"Pardon me for asking this, ma'am, but why haven't I seen you around town?"

"I guess you haven't ever been where I've been at the same time," she teased, "and if you ain't gonna arrest me, then stop calling me ma'am. You can call me Amber."

"Sorry," he blushed, "it's one of those sheriff things that we do. But since I'm not arresting you, Amber, you can call me Kurt."

"I don't get out much, Kurt. Really that's an understatement. I go into town about once a week, and it's pretty much a trip straight there and straight back. It's kind of a drag, really. But that's probably why you haven't seen me around."

"Well, I'm glad we finally crossed paths."

"Hey," she chirped, surprisingly grabbing his hand, "you should come inside. I can heat up some coffee. I mean, I know the storm knocked the power out and all, but I can heat some up on the fireplace. It's freezing cold out here."

"Is Mr. Rockhouse here?"

"Yes. He's in there shuffling around in the dark."

Kurt examined the mansion. A cobblestone walkway completely circled the front lawn. Patches of dead weeds sprouted through stones, randomly along the circle. Rooted within its circumference were five tiny spruce trees. They had been planted in perfect position so that imaginary lines could be drawn from tree to tree, forming a pentagram. A brick wall, approximately seven feet in height, extended from each side of the mansion, across the lawn and well into forest thick. Wiry briar patches dangled over both sides of the wall like skeleton arms. Most of the bricks were chipped and eroded. Yet it remained a successful barricade, entirely blocking view of the backyard. About one hundred feet to the home's left, in front of the brick wall, the garage stood, with two, metal sliding doors and siding made of dark brown cedar.

The mansion faced southward, toward town. Everyone was familiar with the entrance. Few people beheld what stretched past the wall. The siding grayed with age (except for random spots Amber painted) and years of neglect yellowed many of the windows. The mansion's east and west corners were flanked by a three-story column of rooms (the same height as the roof). Large, silver cones sprouted like devil horns from the columns. Without these columns, the house was nothing more than a box, crowned by a triangular attic that spanned the flat roof's center like a Mohawk.

Five spearhead-shaped doors ran side by side along the first story; one on each column and three in the middle. Concrete steps rolled like rigid tongues from the doorways. The central entrance adorned a bronze cathead knocker. Directly above each door, at the second story, Rice Chex shaped windows revealed pitch-blackness from inside. The third story presented a window on each column and a large teardrop shaped glass door in the middle. Beneath the teardrop, a balcony, with railing shaped into uniform Celtic crosses, stretched from column to column, supported from underneath by three steel arches.

"Oh, no," Kurt stuttered, intimidated by the gothic mass before him, "really, I don't want to go inside or anything."

Amber released his hand and hung her head with embarrassment.

"I mean, I'd love to have coffee with you," he recovered, "in fact that's something we should do sometime. I just oughta be close by in town incase anybody were to need me."

"I understand," she said, with her head still bowed, "I'll tell RJ that you might be looking around, back on the mountain. If we see or hear anything, we'll let you know right away."

"You know, y'all are kind of stuck on this mountain, and I'm sure it's rough on Mr. Rockhouse with the power being off and all. If you need anything, why don't you let me take you into town? It's no trouble. The old truck goes good in the snow with those chains on the tires."

"It'll take more than a blizzard to kill that old codger," Amber joked, "but you know, I would like to shoot some pool. Do you shoot pool?"

"Yeah," he slurred, with confusion crinkling those bushy eyebrows, "do you mean right now?"

4.

"I have officially lost my mind," Kurt declared, as the county sheriff's truck inched down Muddy Mountain's icy road.

"Why do you say that?" Amber asked, curled up comfortably in the passenger seat. There were several reasons why this situation would normally worry Amber. Yet she uncharacteristically relaxed in the automobile without a care in the world. Her smile never slipped, even when the truck's tires did. Country music played on the radio, barely loud enough to hear. Amber be-bopped to the beat, as if she was in the front row of a concert, tapping percussion on tight blue jeans, with strawberry curls, spiraling out of her turquoise toboggan, bouncing wildly enough to arouse the scent of cherry shampoo.

"Here I am," Kurt groaned, "the county sheriff, on duty, during a blizzard, heading out to shoot pool with a woman I met twenty minutes ago."

"You're the sheriff. You can do whatever you want."

"It's an election year, honey," Kurt laughed, keeping a snail pace down the mountain with no visible signs of anxiety or concern.

In Appalachia, winter weather is a big deal. Most communities have one, main highway, which folks in other parts of the country would consider normal. A web of narrow, curvy roads branch from the main route, alongside creek banks, over mountaintops, twisting past homes scattered about the hillside. Most of these roads are barely wide enough for two vehicles to pass. Should one lose control, a terrifying tumble over an abysmal cliff awaits.

Wintry conditions require more than simply taking it easy. In other parts of the country, people go on about their business in three or four inches of snow. For those in Appalachia, the same amount of accumulation will result in school being canceled for an entire week. Competent drivers like Sheriff Bochester understand the need for confidence and caution amidst these conditions. He never reacted with reflexes. When the rear end began to slide, he brought it back to equilibrium with a gentle tap of the gas pedal. Breaks were not used at all, unless absolutely necessary. Ahead of them unfurled a road, which appeared incased by glass, descending a mountain that would intimidate even the most skilled skier. The truck creaked and groaned, fighting the forces of ice and gravity.

"This is so amazing," Amber exclaimed, "I seriously cannot believe it. You don't understand, Kurt. If anybody else was driving right now, I would freak out big time and probably jump out of the door, while the truck was still moving. But I am not the least bit scared with you driving."

"This road ain't bad," Kurt yawned, "the mountain goes a long way, but the road ain't steep or curvy. As long as we don't get in a hurry, we'll be fine."

"Don't get all macho on me," Amber teased, "seriously, I'm so calm right now, I could flip through a magazine without even watching the road. You make me feel safe."

"When you're sheriff, you better be able to drive in some sticky spots because, let me tell you, bad guys like to hide in sticky spots."

Kurt wasn't totally exaggerating his confidence. Road crews did a good job of plowing excess snow off the passageways. Thankfully, Muddy Mountain's road descended at a low, steady grade. Chains on the tires helped prevent sliding. Kurt dropped the passenger's side wheels onto gravel beside the asphalt to gain even more traction, and left the engine in first gear, allowing the truck to creep slowly downhill without assistance of breaks. Still, great caution was necessary. More than a foot of snow blanketed the area, and with extra girth added to drifts by the highway crew's plows, a vehicle could easily be buried beneath a mound of snow, if it veered off the cleared path. Muddy Mountain did not present an ideal setting, should this situation occur. All of the elements, which made the place spooky, also rendered it dangerous.

Continuous flowing water had carved deep gullies into roadside ditches, where a vehicle could land on its top, submerging passengers in a frozen mess of muddy slime. Long, razor-sharp icicles dangled like claws from a canopy of dying trees slouching over the road. Each tree bent amidst the weight of ice, its wooden spine cracking; ready at any moment to signal bone crushing demise with a deafening pop and treacherous tumble. Mud coated the mountainside thick enough to bury a vehicle up to its bumpers and pedestrians up to their knees. Hollows and open meadows offered the slow, cold death of drowning in quicksand.

Kurt and Amber were not oblivious to these dangers. Yet they remained calm, driving through the frozen jungle. Amber smiled, and Kurt couldn't help but think about how beautiful she looked. Escapades like this were not the norm for Sheriff Bochester. Amber Rockhouse accomplished what hundreds of pretty women before her could not. She charmed the high-sheriff and played his emotions like a deck of cards. Before Kurt even knew what happened, he and Amber were out on a date in the county vehicle, with a slight hint of lustful anticipation overpowering logic and safety. Maybe it was her hypnotic good looks or the perfect combination of sassy and sweet in her personality, but whatever the reason, Amber Rockhouse possessed a strange power over Kurt Bochester. He just hadn't realized it yet.

Since assuming the office of sheriff, Kurt entertained a few females. One relationship even got serious. They dated for two years. But she loved to pop those little, blue pills. And he, of course, served as the county's top law enforcement official. Needless to say, their relationship didn't work out.

Kurt understood the majesty of marriage and the tragedy of divorce. During the worst year of his life (the year before he became sheriff) Kurt's parents died at the hands of a drunk driver. Two months later, his wife left him. They last spoke to each other at the divorce hearing, ten years ago. Kurt never cried over her. He simply thanked God that they didn't have any children together. Throughout time, love gave him a few high fives along with an abundance of low blows. Such is the case for pretty much everybody. However, not one time did he use his badge as a chick-magnet. The same could not be said for his deputies. They earned a reputation for chasing bad guys by day and chasing bad girls at night, but he never lectured them. A cop's life is always on the line. If his deputies could legally garner a few fringe benefits, so be it. You never know. They might all be dead tomorrow.

Kurt accomplished a lot for a 38 year-old. He loved his work, but there is more to a man than merely a job. Even sheriffs need love. He thought about sex regularly and companionship on occasion. These urges always took a backseat to his greatest passion... law enforcement. Yet from out of the wild, blue yonder, he found himself accidentally engaged in a romantic outing with a hot, young woman, amidst the most unlikely of circumstances. As foolish and impulsive as his day out with Amber might have been, Kurt didn't resist the temptation. She was playful, not in an annoying way, but with a subtle flirtation that made him feel giddy. Sheriffs don't get giddy. But Kurt did every time Amber smiled.

"Thank God," he cried, once they reached the long rows of evergreens, lining the road at Muddy Mountain's entrance, "it took a little while, but we have successfully made it to the bottom of the mountain."

"I'm finally free," Amber howled.

"The road crews have been working hard on clearing ice and snow. The road is still slick but we have flatland from here on out. So, we'll be just fine."

"Great! I'm actually excited."

"I can't go in no bar," Kurt lectured, "not while I'm on duty. Besides, the power is out. So, you have two choices. We can drive up to the pool hall and just hope that some crazy fool came out during a power outage to open the place up. Or we can go to my house. I've got a pool table in the basement. It's up to you."

"Your place will be okay," Amber confirmed, "Ain't nothing like beating a man on his own table."

"I'd give you a clever comeback, if I was any good at playing pool," Kurt grinned, "but I reckon a butt whopping is probably what I'm in for."

Amber never sat the right way in her seat. She fidgeted a lot. Her actions seemed rebellious, like a teenager, who refuses conformity to anything socially standard. Sometimes, she lounged with her back to the door, limberly cradling one foot against her crotch. Then she'd prop her feet on the dashboard or sit Indian style, with the seatbelt still buckled, but tucked behind her back rather than across her chest. She gave no indication that the sheriff's presence intimidated her.

"So, this is a date," Amber said, slightly blushing, "I'm on a date with the sheriff. I would rush home and tell all of my girlfriends, if I had any girlfriends."

"Now, wait a minute," he teased, "I'm on duty. So, this ain't a date. It's just a public service."

"Do you usually ride around and pickup lowly folks in desperate need of a ride to the pool hall?"

"Like I said, it's an election year," Kurt chuckled.

Amber's laugh was pure like she really felt it. Finally, she removed her toboggan, and as laughter spilled so did her curls. The aroma of cherries radiated from everything, her breath, hair, and skin. Kurt found it difficult to drive slowly with his heart beating so fast.

"You take your job too seriously," she criticized.

"When I don't take my job seriously, people die."

"Oh boy," Amber cackled, clapping her hands, "that line belongs in a movie."

"Yeah," Kurt blushed, "that was pretty corny wasn't it?"

"That's okay," she assured, "it's cool to be corny sometimes. But we *are* on a date."

"Good," he answered, "that means I don't have to go through that awkward 'asking you out for the first time' phase."

"No, but we still have to go through that unpredictable 'getting to know you' phase."

"Yep, there's no skipping that one is there?"

"Afraid not."

Past the evergreen rows at Muddy Mountain's entrance, land opened into a vast plain and all of town could be seen. Sugarland sat to the immediate left. Trailers, glazed with ice, twinkled, every color of the prism. Cars in the driveways resembled giant marshmallows, with snow smoothly spread across their hoods, roofs, and trunks. Many of the houses on town's northern tip stood for over a century. Black smoke spiraled from their thin chimneys, filling town with the hearty smell of burning kindling and coal. Municipal buildings formed a miniature skyline. Railroad tracks curved along one side of the river. Main Street mimicked from the opposite side. A post office, bank, water treatment facility, diner, barber shop, fire station, and a handful of high rise office complexes lined like toy soldiers all the way back to the coal tipple, where trains were loaded with black gold, in route to all four corners of the country. Near the base of mountains at the southern end of town's open plain, a shopping center stretched beside the highway. This is where town's pulse became most rapid, with the super market, department stores, movie-theater, bowling alley, and fast food restaurants drawing traffic from natives, as well as folks in adjoining counties. A tiny, white church, high on a mountain behind the shopping center, marked town's southern city limit.

Normally, the highway buzzed with tight traffic during afternoon hours. But the blizzard smothered all life. Windows were black. Both the river and road appeared frozen in mid flow. The shopping center's parking lot shimmered, a solid sheet of white. Outside an occasional plow, Kurt and Amber owned Main Street. They rolled past lonely structures, barely above crawl-speed, chains clanging loudly against asphalt. The scene created an atmosphere both romantic and eerie. On a drive through winter's wonderland, they seized opportunity to break the ice.

"You know, I read something in a magazine that said couples should tell each other their biggest secret on the first date," said Amber, "I guess, if you still like a guy after hearing his biggest secret, the relationship stands a good chance."

"I'm not telling you my biggest secret," Kurt smiled.

"Why not?"

"Because I'm just not gonna do it. We could be married for fifty years and you'd never know."

"Oh my God," Amber gasped, "are you an axe murderer?"

"I'm not an axe murderer."

"Are you gay?"

"No," Kurt snickered, "it's not anything profound. It's just embarrassing."

"My biggest secret is really big."

"Tell me."

"I'm serious," she said with a somber tone, "it's a big one."

"I tell you what. Let's start a little slower. Maybe we should tell each other our third biggest secret."

"Oh geeze," Amber sighed, "I can pick my biggest secret easy. But picking number three is going to be hard."

"You got one?"

"Sure."

"Go ahead," he coaxed.

"No way," she rejected, "you go first."

"Why?"

"Because," she groaned, "you might just make something silly up after you hear my secret."

"There you go," replied Kurt, "we have too many trust issues. I guess we should just play some pool, have a good time, and save the secrets for later."

"Yeah," Amber agreed, "I never believe what I read in magazines."

Kurt's house looked exactly the way Amber pictured it...

- Pointed roof
- Two stories covered with cedar siding
- Red front door
- Covered front porch spanning the entire width of the first story
- Two car garage jutting from the right side of the house
- Concrete driveway leading to the garage

Although the lawn was snow covered, she imagined it to be well kept, with perfectly trimmed bushed buried somewhere beneath the blizzard's blanket. The inside was as neat as a woman could ever expect any single, straight, workingman to keep it. His interior design lacked a woman's touch. But it was obvious that Kurt dusted, mopped, washed dishes, and took care of the laundry on a regular basis. As they pulled into the driveway, Amber thought, "I bet he has a deer head mounted above the fireplace." Sure enough, there it hung- an eleven point buck, stuffed from the neck up and screwed onto a plank, engaged in an eternal stare down with a portrait of Jesus hanging on the adjacent wall.

"Nice head," Amber noted, pointing to the buck above the fireplace.

"That's my buddy," Kurt boasted, "I killed him three years ago with a crossbow. His name is King Louie. I've got Marie Antoinette hanging in the den."

One word to describe the house... RUSTIC! Everything was made of wood-furniture, floors, walls, and even the decorations. Amber expected to walk into the bathroom and see a wooden toilet. There are certain lines not even the most avid wood lover will cross. To Amber's surprise, Kurt's toilets were made of porcelain. Naturally, if it were Amber's home, she would make many changes. Yet she really liked the house. In fact, she thought it was awesome. Kurt did a pretty good job... for a man.

"You know what the funny thing about this house is?" Kurt said, as they finished the tour, "I didn't build it until after my divorce. My ex wife got half the value of the singlewide trailer we lived in while we were married. That's some sweet justice. EJ lives here with me, but when he's here, he stays hidden in the basement. Eventually... maybe, he'll move out. This is a little bit too much house for a single man."

"If you want to see too much house, come inside my place," she dared, "I live in that mansion with two men, and unless we eat breakfast or supper together, I don't see them or hear them all day long."

"At least you have privacy."

"I guess so, but that place makes me worry sick about Big Daddy. If he is in one of the far rooms and he calls out for help, we'll never hear him. He'd lay there croaked for probably at least a whole day before anyone found him."

Kurt led Amber downstairs. The basement air was so cold they could see their breath. EJ turned the space into a quaint apartment. A small kitchen area, with refrigerator and stove crammed into a corner, sat at one end of the long room. A pool table, dusty blue sofa, and a few folding chairs occupied the middle space. With the electricity out, the only light came from a small window above the sofa. The light was dim but sufficient enough to see all around. At the far end, one door led to EJ's bedroom, which consisted of a mattress on the floor with blankets bunched up in the center, a television, also on the floor, and assortments of clothing scattered about chaotically. The other door opened to the bathroom. EJ obviously decorated the basement with furniture and accessories that had been given to him throughout time. Nothing matched.

"You've gotta look over the basement," Kurt griped, setting flame to the wick of a kerosene heater, "I pretty much leave EJ alone down here. I'm surprised it isn't in worse shape than this."

"Don't worry, honey," Amber comforted, "our mansion stays a bloody mess."

"Can I ask you a personal question?" Kurt pried, racking balls on the pool table.

"You can ask whatever question you want," Amber mocked, "and I'll give you whatever answer I want."

"How much money does old RJ have?"

"Let me tell you," she laughed, chalking her cue, "he has a lot! The lottery ain't ever offered any kind of jackpot like Big Daddy's got stashed. I know he has millions. I'm not sure exactly how much, but I'm pretty sure it's closer to one billion than it is to one million."

"Good God almighty," Kurt exclaimed with a whistle, "you ought to be wiping your rump with two-ply gold."

"There is one good thing I can say about Big Daddy," she answered, striking the cue ball into a beautiful break, "he's never been stingy with me when it comes to money. I guess he feels guilty over everything else, so he tries to compensate with cash. But I've never wanted for anything. I could make one phone call and have a Ferrari in your driveway by tomorrow morning."

"My phone is on the couch," Kurt joked.

"But you know, Kurt, what they say is true. Money can't buy you happiness. I know some folks would want to choke me if they heard me say that, but it's true."

"I understand what you're saying," he assured, looking the table over, trying to figure out how he got so far behind on only the break, "I've had happy times in my life, and none of them were happy because of money. I've had plenty of unhappy times too, and I tell you, no amount of money in the world could have made those days any better."

Amber knocked balls into the pockets with such speed and precision, Kurt thought she might be cheating. He couldn't figure out how, but cheating is the only explanation for a display like Amber put on. Occasionally, she tried something silly like a behind the back shot with her eyes closed. Kurt knew she was doing that on purpose so he would have a chance to shoot. Each turn for Kurt consisted of about five minutes of aiming, ten seconds of balls scattering wildly, hitting every part of the table except the pockets, and then about two minutes of intense cursing.

"Just relax, Kurt," Amber scolded, "getting beat by a girl isn't such a bad thing. That gives you incentive to practice."

"I ain't got time to practice," he grumbled.

"Well then, I guess you have a good excuse."

There was a moment of silence, while Kurt measured out his shot, hoping to redeem at least a little dignity. Already, Amber had him on the squirm. The little boy in Kurt was angry that a girl could beat him. But the full-grown man in Kurt was kind of turned on. Amber stared off into space, inattentively grinding a cube of chalk against the tip of her cue, while little boy Kurt and full-grown Kurt battled for control of his emotions.

"Honey, it's tough to make a shot like that off the rail," she criticized, "your best bet would be to just hit the cue ball as hard as you can."

"Amber," he joked, "shut up. I'm thinking instead of playing pool, we should just arm wrestle."

Kurt's chance at redemption ended with disaster- another shot gone horribly wrong. His temper boiled hotter with every stroke of the cue. Until that moment, Amber laughed at all of his botched shots. This time she remained quiet. The look on her face indicated that she was lost in deep concentration on something other than the game. Amber slumped over to take her shot and in the same instant arose back to full posture, gently sat her cue on the table, and slowly sifted pink fingernails through strawberry hair.

"Can we step out on the porch?" she whined, beginning to tremble.

"I guess so. Are you okay?"

Amber tried to breathe without gasping. The basement became a vacuum, and slender walls tightened around her like a boa constrictor. "Not now. Please, not right now," she thought.

All efforts to maintain control were useless. Her attacks usually came with warning and built up to a climax. This time, however, panic hit hard, within the blink of an eye. Amber knew the collapsing sensation was all in her head, but the loss of breath was very much reality. Unless she made it outside soon, the date would come to an end with puke all over Kurt's floor.

She stammered upstairs without answering Kurt and frantically staggered to the front door, choking and quaking, cold sweat running down her cheeks. On the porch, she immediately collapsed into a rocking chair, buried her face in her hands, and wept.

"Oh my God, Amber," Kurt panted, sprinting behind her, "are you okay? What's wrong?"

"Me," she sobbed, "that's what's wrong."

"Did I do something?"

"No," she answered, laughing and crying at the same time, as she uncovered her face, "that attack didn't give me any warning. I'm a little bit claustrophobic."

"Oh," he moaned, sounding relieved, "I'm sorry. I guess the basement isn't the best place for that, is it?"

"I'm the one who's sorry. Jesus, this is so embarrassing."

Kurt stepped in front of her and leaned back against the

railing. Lines of frustration webbed across her forehead. She fidgeted in the seat; trembling hands unable to stay still. Strands of hair clung to wet cheeks. Embarrassed eyes stared at the porch floor. She appeared so sad and frightened. Kurt's heart melted with the sight of Amber's struggle.

"Stop crying, now," he soothed, wondering whether or not he should hug her, "Let me ask you something. Are you afraid of spiders?"

"No," she said, wiping tears away.

"Well, I am. It's not just regular fear either. It's an all out phobia. I panic when I see one. I won't even get close enough to kill them."

"Okay," she did not seem comforted.

"You don't understand. I'll start hyperventilating and screaming if one gets on me. Now, if that had happened to me in there, I'd feel the same way you do right now."

She smiled.

"Don't you be one bit sad, Amber. Everything is just fine."

Countless times, Kurt stood before vulnerable women. Some cried when he pulled them over. Others prattled nervously, flirted, or simply froze. Amber, however, displayed vulnerability, there on the porch, unfamiliar to Kurt. Her frowning eyes and quivering lips revealed a desperate inward battle; a struggle to be free rather than an effort to gain sympathy. When she smiled, her face shined joyfully pretty. Amidst a frown, she became tragically beautiful; sexy, regardless of emotion.

"I'm ready to tell you," she somberly spoke.

"Okay," Kurt replied, "what is it you want to tell me?"

"My third biggest secret."

"You mean, this isn't it?"

"No," she laughed.

"Let's hear it."

She closed her legs tightly and sat firm postured in the rocking chair; brow crinkling, as she sucked a redeeming breath through puckered lips. With nervous hands anchored against knees, she closed water filled eyes and confessed at near whisper,

"I'm not happy."

Emerald eyes opened, as her posture relaxed. Amber appeared to have dropped the world's weight from her shoulders. She fell back in the chair, so overcome with relief, a pleasurable moan seeped from her throat like a burp.

"Most days," she continued, "I'm chipper and upbeat and positive, but that's just my nature. Deep inside, I am very unhappy. You're the first person to hear this."

"It's okay," he comforted, "I'm listening, honey."

She smoothed hair away from her face and leaned forward in the rocking chair, speaking barely loud enough for him to hear, as if the trees were spies.

"Kurt, I know you've seen some crazy things in your line of work, but you have never seen anything like what goes on at the top of that mountain. My life is different than anyone else's. Trust me, it's horrible."

"Is there illegal activity going on up there?"

"No, no, no," she quickly responded, "please don't misunderstand me. I love RJ with all my heart. But every night at bedtime, I lie beneath the covers, scared out of my mind that I will not wake up the next morning."

"It's that butler isn't it?" Kurt growled, "Does he get violent with you?"

"No, Kurt, it isn't like that. Don't start playing sheriff, just listen to me, okay? When I was a teenager, all I wanted in the world was to get out and make some friends; kids my age I could talk to. But I never had that. RJ keeps me boxed in that mansion like a rat in a cage. Sure, I can leave every now and then, like right now, but I always have to pay for it, and there's no way he would allow it to happen a lot."

Kurt kneeled on one knee and softly brushed his fingers up and down her shin, with bright, blue eyes smiling beneath bushy brows of grain.

"Amber, baby, you're a grown woman. How old are you?"

"I'm twenty-six."

"Oh," he grimaced, "we'll talk about how old I am later."

"Kurt, I know where you're going with this, and you're right. I am a grown woman, and I should be in charge of my own life. But my life is more complicated than you could ever understand."

"Try me," he insisted.

"As far as my time in the mansion goes, I've pretty much raised myself. RJ has been a really old man for longer than you and I have been alive. He just never had the energy, mentally or physically, for dealing with a teenager."

"Well then, it seems to me that instead of being too sheltered, you would have been too unattended."

"No, Kurt, there's much more to the story. I have been alone throughout all of my time in the mansion, but I have not been free."

"Baby, I'm listening to you, but there's just one thing I'd like to say. You wanted to come with me today, so you did it. I think freedom has a lot to do with taking the first step. If you want to get out, you've just got to take that leap from the nest."

"Maybe I should put it like this," she sighed, leaning back in the chair, "RJ Rockhouse is a mortal being. Sure he's lived ninety-nine years, but all ninety-nine of those years show on his face and in his actions. Much sooner than later, he is going to die."

"So, you feel guilty about leaving him because you're afraid he'll die while you're gone."

"Sort of. Poor, old guy, he has millions of dollars but not many friends, other than Benjamin and me. He'll be turning one hundred soon, and I know he wants to see that birthday."

"I'll tell you something," Kurt chuckled, "if all of this is your third biggest secret, I don't know if I want to hear one and two."

"I'm sorry, Kurt. Listen, I'm not going to bog you down with dreary details of my life or get all... well, the way I get. I mean, this is just a casual get together."

"Seriously, everything is okay," Kurt soothed, "crazy chicks are good in bed, so we'll be just fine... I'm kidding by the way."

"Crazy chicks have to be good in bed or else they'd never get a man. But anyway, I'm not trying to move super fast or freak you out or anything. I just want to say this, and then I'll get back to stomping your ass at pool. There are a lot of beautiful, fascinating women out there, who would love to go out on a date with the sheriff. But if you do want a second date with me or a third or whatever, you should prepare yourself to deal with a girl who is different."

"If you knew the women I've had, being different wouldn't seem like such a flaw."

"Okay," she chirped, "timeout is over."

Amber arose from the chair. All shaking and crying ended as abruptly as it began.

"Will you be okay going back down in the basement?" Kurt asked, rising to offer assistance.

"Usually, my heart speeds up a little and I start sweating, so I know it's time to get out. This time it caught me off guard. Just leave the door open, and if I get to feeling anxious, I'll come outside."

"Let the butt whoopin' commence," Kurt groaned.

"I'll tell you another secret," Amber whispered, as she passed, "I'm a really bored girl, who has a pool table at home. You'll probably never beat me."

They played five games of pool. She humiliated him in every round. Suddenly, Kurt remembered that he was sheriff and his deputies had been alone in the office for most of the day. So, he drove Amber back up Muddy Mountain, through the ice and snow. On the way, they talked about a little bit of everything. There was no kiss or even a holding of hands to seal this union. However, he did ask for her number and pledged an evening call, unless unforeseen sheriff business beckoned him to the rescue.

As Kurt slowly descended Muddy Mountain for the second time that day, he reflected upon the sexy, untamed girl who fell into his house with the fiery suddenness of a meteor. She certainly was interesting. He had no intension of ever calling her.

5.

Arthur sat alone at home, drinking beer on the sofa. He already had a buzz and it was only nine in the morning. Night crew usually clocked out around 7 AM. Arthur arrived home no later than 7:30. His friend, Stevie, gave him a ride in his four-wheel drive Jeep. Straight through the front door, he made a B-line for the bathroom, trading his work uniform for sweat pants and a thermal shirt. Chef Boyardee, Aunt Jemima, and that creepy guy on the Pringles can welcomed Arthur home with a smile. Only one could excel to the coveted status of chow time entrée. Chef Boyardee reigned victorious. Without electricity, Arthur had no choice but to eat his ravioli cold. He could not figure out if the meal was breakfast or supper. It came at 7:45 AM, which society deems breakfast time. But it also served as his post work meal, which society deems to be supper. Following much meditation on the subject, he concluded that it really didn't matter. Chow time typically consisted of processed meat on a stick or a Tupperware bowl full of pasta-like substance, which is hardly considered food, let alone a meal.

Usually a shower followed breakfast/supper/whatever you call it. Arthur chose to postpone all showers until either he became too skanky to tolerate himself or the electricity came back on. The luxuriousness of hot water was something he did not appreciate until it was gone. Thankfully, Arthur had enough foresight to bring a kerosene heater and jug of fuel during the move. The temperature inside was not cozy, but the heater at least kept it from being frigid.

On mornings following busy nights at the store, Arthur hit the hay by nine o'clock. Most days he at least tried to be in bed before noon. Should sleep elude him, beer helped the morning melt away.

That is how life goes for those pulling the graveyard shift. Everything is backwards and confusing. The day changed while Arthur was at work. Most of the time he thought it was

Thursday, although in reality Friday morning had arrived. At other times he thought Thursday evening was Friday because he went to sleep Thursday morning, and in the normal world, a man wakes to a day different from the one he fell asleep in. Day shifters are probably confused by these scenarios. The truth is, night shifters are confused by them, too. Yet somehow they adapt to a dimension where meals have no names and an eight-hour work shift serves as both the ending and beginning of a day.

Each shift presents pros and cons for workers. Arthur liked that the store closed at midnight and did not reopen until 6 AM. This meant he only had to deal with customers for one hour at the beginning of his shift and one hour at the end. Arthur's crew stayed busy, which was good. Time moved quicker for him when there was a lot of work to do. For most of his shift, the only boss in the store was night crew's manager. All the boys on night crew were good friends and hard workers, so they rarely took heat from the suits.

Arthur did not like his salary. He barely earned above minimum wage. With the way raises were set up for night crew, it would be years before his pay increased enough to notice. He hated being tired all the time. Many night shifters suffer from exhaustion due to lack of sleep. Arthur either slept too little during the day or too much. He never went to bed at nine and slept until five. Either he went to bed at nine and slept until noon or he went to bed at nine and slept until time to get ready for work, about 10 PM.

Overall, however, Arthur liked his job with "Town Grocery", though he thought the store's name sounded kind of bland. Seven stores made up the Town Grocery chain, all of them located in southeast Kentucky. Workers felt comfortable with the corporation. It wasn't too large to care about its employees, but it wasn't too small to keep up with the competition. Arthur would have been satisfied working there another thirty years, if he could snag an upper management position. Those jobs paid as well as a southeast Kentucky boy could expect to make without holding a college degree or crawling back into a coalmine.

Arthur devoted more thought to money now that he lived with Judith. Before she came along, cash posed no concern. As long as he had enough to pay the bills and buy some beer, everything was cool by his standards. Women, however, eventually desire a little more from their finances than paying the bills and buying some beer. For the time being, lot #1 of Sugarland trailer park indulged in a bountiful harvest of happiness and hope. Arthur had no idea how long the current supply of cash would meet his girlfriend's growing demand.

Judith woke up at 10:30. She smoked a cigarette and spent about fifteen minutes snuggling Arthur on the couch. The highway department finally cleared the road from Sugarland into town well enough to suit the girls. Judith and Shirley nearly lost their minds with excitement. Now, they were free. Although most stores and restaurants were likely without electricity, the girls harbored hope that civilization stirred somewhere on the far horizon. Town Grocery operated on generated power through the storm. If all else failed, they would go grocery shopping. The girls didn't care. They simply longed to be anywhere other than home. Arthur already felt a sting in his wallet and they had yet to leave the trailer park.

He had never seen a girl get ready so fast. Judith called Shirley and within ten minutes, hair and teeth were brushed, clothes were on, and the girls hit asphalt. With no TV or radio, Arthur stripped down to his underwear and quickly fell asleep beneath blankets on the couch.

Just then (wouldn't you know it?) somebody knocked on the front door. He stumbled through the living room and kitchen, frantically searching for his shirt and pants. Murphy's Law states that if one is at risk of being caught with his pants down, his pants will become impossible to find. The knocking continued, this time with urgent force and impatient rhythm. Arthur's clothes had somehow shuffled beneath the end table.

He hastily dressed and answered the door in a fury. Curse words so foul they make sailors cringe, boiled like lava in Arthur's throat. But the roaring lion of lot #1 retreated to nothing more than a meek, little lamb, when his den's door opened to reveal a man so thick he blocked all light, with shoulders, legs, and fists carved of stone. This mammoth man/creature did not look down as Arthur opened the door. Instead, he held stationary position with beady, black eyes locked straight ahead. The decrepit giant rendered not the slightest twitch. A more perfect mannequin had never been molded. For Arthur, this scene served as the exact replica of a nightmare so accurately, for a brief second, he thought he was asleep.

During childhood, a reoccurring nightmare continually vexed Arthur's slumber. Throughout that series of dreams, the setting occasionally changed. The plot and characters, however, remained the same. A large man, with a squared head and green complexion, reminiscent of Frankenstein's monster, chased young Arthur. Sometimes, the prowler jumped from a closet. Once, Arthur caught him peeping through the window of his bedroom. Most times, he chased Arthur down an empty street. One purpose fueled the persistence of this ghoulish assailant. He feigned for the taste of Arthur's thumbs. The stalker's crazed pleas for just one morsel of Arthur's tender thumb echoed within his nightmares the way a demon's laughter echoes in horror movies.

Sometimes, the stalker successfully captured him. Suffocating within the goon's python grip, Arthur's arms flailed in fearful attempt to protect his thumbs from the rotting, drool slicked razor points jaggedly lining the fiend's chomping jaws. Peril seemed inevitable. But, as the brute's slimy tongue slithered across the tip of Arthur's helpless thumb, he awoke from the nightmare. Lying fully alert in bed, his heart raced and sweat drenched the pillow, but both thumbs remained intact.

These dreams continued until the day Arthur turned ten. The very night of his tenth birthday, Arthur once again dreamed of his thumb hungry foe. This time, however, rather than fleeing down an empty street, Arthur engaged the bully in a sword fight. A swashbuckling series of fencing maneuvers ensued, until finally Arthur's cunning swordsmanship rendered the perfect opportunity for victory. With one mighty swing, he decapitated the giant and never dreamed of him again.

Now, there he stood, wearing the same faded black coat and rust colored shirt; his thick jaw and broad forehead faintly tinted green. Arthur did not know what to say. So, he stood in silence for several seconds. The man did not introduce himself or offer any greeting. Instead, he slowly rotated on his heels away from the door like a large stone uncovering a tomb's entrance. The gesture reminded Arthur of the way a creepy butler welcomed guests into a home in old, black and white scary movies. Once he rolled completely away from the opening, it became obvious that the man was indeed a butler; the infamous butler of RJ Rockhouse.

Arthur had never met his landlord, yet he knew that the frail figure, slumped over and trembling at the end of his porch, could be none other than RJ. There he stood in all his magnificent macabre. Rockhouse, the myth, the legend, the terrifying reality, cowered from merely feet away. A black shawl whipped in winter wind. Lily skin dripped in wrinkles from his bones, as if melting. RJ was everything Arthur expected and more. His eyes were the color of winter sky. A few dry strands of silver hair sprouted in random spots from Rockhouse's pink scalp like tassel. All in all, RJ stood five feet tall and weighed less than an egg. Yet he was the most intimidating being Arthur ever saw.

"Arthur Adler?" Rockhouse gurgled. His voice was coarse and toneless, making it impossible to determine if he was happy, agitated, or simply content.

"Yes, sir," Arthur answered.

"I'm RJ Rockhouse."

Corn colored claws bitterly tapped the diamond head of an ebony cane. His jagged, icicle smile held constant like that of a skull.

"Is everything okay with your trailer?"

"Yes, sir, we appreciate what you have done for us here."

"I need to talk to you for a minute, if that's okay."

"Sure."

"Before I come into the house, I need to know if there are any cloves of garlic, crucifixes, or wooden stakes in there that could hurt me."

Rockhouse's tone remained dry, which was such an odd contrast to his skull-like smile. Arthur's eyes widened and he lost his breath for a second.

"I'm only kidding, Arthur," Rockhouse assured, with his monotone grainy voice, "can I come in?"

"Of course," Arthur blushed, "please come in."

Rockhouse scampered into the trailer like a mouse and looked from side to side without pivoting his head. He wiggled on Popsicle legs to the lip of the sofa. Rusty joints creaked as he lowered himself to the seat.

"Don't worry," Rockhouse grunted, "I'm not here to check up on you. This place is yours. You can do whatever you want with it. I just want to talk to you about something important."

"Sure," Arthur replied, choosing to stand on the opposite end of the living room.

"Benjamin, you may leave us now. Wait in the vehicle and help me down those steps when I'm ready to leave, please."

Benjamin turned and walked away with the grace of a robot, closing the door behind.

"You live here with a young lady named Judith, right?"

"That's right, sir."

Rockhouse pointed to a prom picture, framed on top the entertainment center.

"Is that a picture of her?"

"Yes, sir, it is."

"She's a pretty girl. Is she here right now?"

"No, sir. They have the road clear. So, she's gone into town."

"Women love to shop," Rockhouse grumbled, "I have an adopted daughter. She's ordered a tanning bed for the mansion; a tanning bed for Christ's sake. That's what I love about capitalism, Arthur. Give a capitalist enough time and he'll figure out how to charge you for sunshine. Well, I'm glad you're alone. I kind of want this talk to be between me and you."

"Yes, sir."

Arthur realized he was repeating himself, but was afraid to say anything other than "yes, sir". Rockhouse looked almost unreal. He trembled, as if freezing. His movements were choppy like those of a puppet. Flabby skin jiggled on the bone with every twitch; that greasy smile never retreating. Arthur got the sense that nothing could startle RJ- a loud clasp of thunder, a rabid dog, a chainsaw wielding madman. He peered about the room inquisitively, yet seemed completely comfortable.

"I'm preparing my last will and testament," Rockhouse stated, "the mansion and a little bit of money will go to somebody. Each lot and trailer here will go to the family living in it. All the rest of my money is going to be willed to you."

A series of half words followed by coughs and wheezes exploded from Arthur. Had he been a cartoon, his eyes would have popped out and his tongue would have rolled to the floor. As embarrassing as this might have been, he could not control the overwhelming surge of surprise and emotion. Finally, he captured enough self-control to bark, "Can I ask why?"

"I'm going to tell you why," Rockhouse continued, showing no reaction (sympathetic or annoyed) to Arthur's episode, "There is something you will have to do for it."

"I imagine there would be," Arthur nervously giggled.

"I'm turning one hundred soon. On the day I turn a hundred, I want you to kill me."

Just when Arthur got his coughing fit under control, along came another eye popping, tongue rolling revelation that sent him into aftershock.

"Kill you?" he wheezed.

"Yes," Rockhouse confirmed, "I'm having it put in my will that I don't want any autopsies or blood work done on me. I'll tell them it goes against my religion or some crap like that. Still, I don't think you should shoot me or do anything too bloody. That'll just draw suspicion and lead to an investigation. If I was you, I'd smother me with a pillow or something."

With that being said, Rockhouse labored to rise from the sofa. His arm jiggled as if filled with pudding, as he steadied himself on the cane. Slowly he shuffled along the floor. Throughout all of the conversation, his tone presented no more emotion than one would possess asking a friend for a ride into town. This entire episode appeared "normal" to RJ.

"When the will is finalized," he panted in mid shuffle, "I'll give you the exact dollar amount that you will receive."

"Mr. Rockhouse..."

"Stop it," Rockhouse demanded, maintaining a low pitch tone, "I know what you're going to say. This is the part of the conversation where you say, 'I could never do something like that, Mr. Rockhouse.' Or, 'Life is precious. You should cherish every second of it, Mr. Rockhouse.' I do not have many breaths remaining, Arthur. I can't afford to waste any. So, let's cut this part of the conversation, okay? Let me say it like this. If you kill me on my 100th birthday, you will inherit roughly half a billion dollars. That's billion with a B. For a price that high, somebody will kill me if you don't. But if you chose not to kill me on my 100th birthday, you should know that I am willing your lot and trailer to somebody else."

"Mr. Rockhouse," Arthur pleaded, boldly stepping between RJ and the door, "can I please ask why you chose me for this?"

Rockhouse clasped the shawl at the center of his bony breast with frail, trembling fingers. His breaths were gurgles. Every blink seemed to take great effort. He was a short, weak man, with wobbling bones, doughy liver spots, and aspirations for nothing more than the grave. Yet his presence demanded strict reverence. Each glance shattered stone.

"This place started with thirteen trailers," he spoke at near whisper, "Did you know that?"

"No, sir."

"When I opened the place, there were people fighting over trailers. It was almost a riot. This upset me because I wanted to make people happy, not mad or disappointed. So, I upped the number to fifty and invited everyone back. But the second time was the opposite. Instead of not enough trailers, there was one too many... this one. Lot number one was the misfit. Nobody chose it. So, I decided that whoever moved into this lot would become a lottery winner. That's you, Arthur. You've won the lottery."

Arthur gave no verbal reply. He simply nodded and moved out of Mr. Rockhouse's way. RJ opened the door and carefully crunched onto ice, accumulated on the front porch. He turned to flash Arthur one last evil grin.

"I know this is a lot to dump on somebody all at once. You'll need time to calm down and think about it. You have until one week from today to give me your answer. Please, tell your girlfriend I said hello, and I hope she enjoys the book I gave her. Good day, Arthur."

6.

Intensions and actions are two different energies. Kurt honestly intended to ignore Amber. However, he kicked intensions to the curb and called her anyway. Amber spoke truth the day they played pool. There probably were women in town, desiring a date with the sheriff. One tiny problem existed. Kurt didn't want to go out with any of them. The women he dated were either too wild or not wild enough. Discovering *Baby Bear's porridge* seemed hopeless. Perhaps that is why he found Amber so attractive. He could not read her.

Her looks didn't help matters. She was an absolute doll. With every spare second, fantasies flickered in Kurt's head of Amber, bare before a mirror, brushing her strawberry hair; electric waves of timid seduction shining in her eyes. Then she moves to the lawn and does a striptease on a trampoline, her hair shimmering with tiny crystals of ice falling from the wintry breeze. These fantasies are a curse to men. But should the fantasies become reality, there is no greater blessing, even in Heaven.

Kurt's continual fantasies paled in comparison to Amber's obsession. Amber never had anything (let alone anyone) to do. She plundered about the mansion all day and night, grief-stricken with longing for the sheriff. The way he made her feel safe, his rustic mystique, everything about him, including the tiny imperfections, controlled all thought. For the second time in her existence, Amber had taken a great fall.

Only two days passed since they met. Yet suspense paralyzed her. Every slow tick of the clock brought a seesaw of emotions. "He loves me. He loves me not." So, when Amber answered her cell phone and heard Kurt's voice, it was a definitive moment of exhilaration for both of them. There is nothing more exciting and frightening than the *getting to know you* phase.

"Kurt," she cried, embarrassed by her impulsive, excited reaction.

"Hey, Amber, was you busy?"

"Oh yeah," she laughed, "you caught me counting tiles in the bathroom. It's a dull day as usual in the mansion."

Amber had actually been pulling heads off some of her dolls and matching them up with better bodies, but she didn't figure that was the kind of information one revealed before the first kiss.

"You rich folks and your extravagant lifestyle," he teased, "Listen, I'm sorry I didn't call you the other night."

"It's okay," she pouted, "I figured you'd be busy sheriffin' and all."

"Yeah."

He didn't mention that he actually intended to ignore her. That wasn't the kind of information one revealed before the first kiss.

"I thought about you this morning. I wanted to call you then."

"Why didn't you?"

"It was 6:30 in the morning. Only crazy people like me get up that early when the power is out."

"Wow," she marveled, "I'm not even that crazy."

"I just need someone to talk to," he sighed, "and well, you're the one I want it to be."

"Okay, talk to me."

"I will, but for now there is something I want to do, and I want you to be the one to do it with me."

"Why sheriff," she exclaimed, "you go from no kiss on the first date, straight into turbo gear."

"No, no, I didn't mean that," although he didn't think it was a bad idea, "I want you to go dancing with me. But I've got to warn you. I'm out of practice. It's been probably fifteen years since I went dancing, and I wasn't very good at it back then."

"So, let's see," she said, poking fun, "on the first date, we play pool, which you suck at. On the second date, we go dancing, which you suck at. Let me guess. You're not trying to impress me."

"Hey now," he defended, "I'm being sweet. You told me your third biggest secret, but I never told you mine. So, I'm gonna show you. My third biggest secret is I love to dance, but I ain't any good at it. If my deputies found out, life would be hell, let me tell you."

"Ahhh, how precious. Your secret is safe with me. Now, what did you have in mind? Is the sheriff gonna go to a bar, or do you have a dance floor at your house?"

"The bars around here are too redneck and sleazy," he groaned, "Besides that, who knows how long it will be before they get the electricity back on. I figure we could go to a real club in Lexington."

"Ahhh, is the sheriff afraid to be seen in town with a hot, young girl?"

"No, it's not like that, I swear. I tell you what. If you want, on the way out of town, we can stop in the middle of Main Street and I'll pull out my bullhorn and tell everybody we're going out on a date."

"Don't get so defensive," she lectured, "I'm just playing with you. Listen, honey, I might be rich and pretty, but I'm still the daughter of RJ Rockhouse. We can just lay low and have fun while you go through this election. Seriously, I'm cool with that."

Kurt really needed to hear that from her.

"Well, when are you available?" he asked.

Amber knew she would have to sneak out.

"Anytime you want," she confirmed.

Amber sneaked out easily. Staying gone for a long period of time could pose a problem, should RJ need her for anything and realize she was absent. Amber did not care. She never truly realized how boring her life was until Kurt sparked excitement. Now, she itched, yearned, NEEDED to be away from that mansion.

Kurt picked her up about a quarter of the way off the mountain. At that distance, RJ would not hear or see the vehicle. It embarrassed Amber to sneak out like a teenager. For Kurt, however, the situation made him feel young. The roads were somewhat clear, but snow remained on the mountains. Temperatures failed to rise above freezing, even with afternoon sun beaming down. The drive to Lexington consumed two hours. Along the way, Appalachia's mountains melt into the rolling knolls of central Kentucky's Bluegrass Region. It is a beautiful drive, perfect for "getting to know each other".

"What a year," Kurt sighed, rubbing his head, "what a month."

"You've got a lot on your mind."

"Yes I do. I don't think I've ever been so stressed out."

"Tell me all about it."

"EJ picked a fine time to pull his crap. I swear to God, I'm gonna kill him."

"He'll come back."

"I know he's not wrecked anywhere in the county. I can't get him on his cell phone, but the power outage has messed up some folks' service. I can't get a hold of his girlfriend either, but that's good. That probably means they've gone off somewhere together."

"He'll be back just as good as new."

"I'm thinking about kicking him out of the house. I'll have to give him a load of money to help him get on his feet, but I can't handle worrying over him anymore. As long as he's at the house, his irresponsibility is right in my face."

"Sometimes, I wish RJ would kick me out of the house."

Amber stared out across an ocean of white. She thought of the snowman, standing strong and proud on the forest's border. While all other creatures cursed winter's frigid air, the snowman raised slender twig arms toward Heaven, as if praising God for granting one more, frosty day of existence. His glee would be short lived. A week is a long life for snowmen. God's grace might hold for a few days, but inevitably the thermometer rises above thirty-two, and everything snowy (including men) melts into mud. Amber couldn't help but fear that Kurt was another snowman. Joy and fear battled in her heart. As exciting and new as it was, she dreaded the "getting to know you" phase because this meant she had to let Kurt inside her mind. How could he understand her if she couldn't even understand herself? Looking at the snow made her want to run through it in a bikini; wallowing until it paralyzed her skin, with frigid, wet hair biting her face like a snake. She craved these things, and she didn't know why.

Equal insecurities mounted Kurt's expectations. Amber could not comprehend the crushing anxiety of a political campaign. He loved the people and hated them with uniform passion. Voters granted his greatest dream. Yet as sure as moths ignorantly kamikaze into a candle's open flame, voters hold the power and possibility of electing Bozo the clown as next sheriff. Legacies are built with actions. Campaigns are built with bullshit. Voters are sheep and propaganda is the shepherd. He really worried about the upcoming election.

"Then there's this election," Kurt continued, "You know what kills me about my job? I have devoted 100% to the county for over eight years. We've made communities safer and taken drug dealers off the streets. But I can still be without a job, come Election Day, losing to somebody with not even one day of law enforcement experience."

"It's a long way to the May primary," she comforted.

"Politicians make laws but they stink when it comes to enforcing them. But sheriff is a political job. I hate that."

"The people elected you twice. They must like what you're doing."

"It all sort of fell in my lap," he whined, "Buddy Campbell was sheriff before me. His wife got cancer with one year left in his sixth term. He went ahead and retired. When a sheriff retires, it is the county judge-executive's job to appoint a new one. Judge Rose owed Sheriff Campbell some favors. He got me appointed. I did a good enough job in that one year to get elected to a full term. The second time around, nobody ran against me. This time I'm facing John Spencer. He's from the southern end of the county. I'm from the north. The whole election comes down to the middle of the county."

"Do they like you there?"

"You tell me. People lie to politicians. He has an advantage I don't have."

"What's that?"

"He's never been sheriff."

"Yeah, honey, but he has a disadvantage, too."

"And what would that be?"

"He's not you."

"God, woman," he chuckled, "you're gonna be the death of me. But I tell you what, I'm sure gonna have fun dying."

Kurt couldn't stop smiling. A natural comfort existed between them, even during long moments of silence. They passed priceless images along the way. Near the county line, a tiny mutt bobbed up and down across a snowy field, like a dolphin flipping in and out of water, leaving a puppy-width trench along its trek. A few miles down the road, a man scraped ice from his minivan's windshield, wearing a tank top, boxer shorts, flip flops, and a scarf wrapped around his neck. Sometimes, they laughed and chit chatted. Other moments were quiet and dull. Regardless, both of them smiled and relaxed contently like a couple, who had been together for a long while.

"I'm going to crack the window just a little, if that's okay," Amber said, appearing slightly pale.

"Sure. Are you feeling alright?"

"Yes. If I start getting anxious, I'll let you know and we can stop somewhere, for a minute. I'm okay right now, but we have got to change this music," she already had her fingers on the dial, "I'm in a damn good mood, and I want to hear some rock 'n' roll."

"Baby, if rock 'n' roll makes you shake that cute, little behind, then I say crank it."

"That's my man," she whaled, stopping on her favorite station, "I just love rock 'n' roll. It can be sinister yet spiritual. It can be simple yet abstract. It can be soft or hard, but either way, it gives you a good beat to bump to in bed."

"I've always been a country music man. I like simple songs about everyday life that I can relate to."

"Don't be a square," she scolded, punching him on the arm, "rock 'n' roll is where it's at, baby. But some rock bands are kind of stupid. I seen this flyer one time for a concert this rock band was doing. The name of the band was Chainsaw Abortion. Can you believe that name? Those guys must be idiots."

"That is pretty morbid," Kurt grimaced.

"Pretty morbid," she gasped, "now, that would be a cool name for a rock 'n' roll band. But Chainsaw Abortion is thoughtless. I betcha those guys picked that name because they thought it was cool. I'd like to hear what they would say if they ever came face to face with a woman who'd had an abortion. I bet they'd freeze like a deer in headlights."

"You're in a saucy mood today," Kurt chuckled.

"You are the poison, baby."

Amber did a good job fighting off anxiety. Every now and then, her face faded pale and her eyes slanted with worry. These bouts lasted a few minutes, until a song she liked played on the radio, snapping her back into cheery spirits. The drive would have been a little easier for her during spring, when the terrain popped with a plethora of color. In the blizzard's aftermath, everything appeared closed in and lifeless. But Amber was actually proud of herself. She successfully fought off suffocation with everything she had. Whenever Kurt noticed her turning pale, he tried to chase away an attack with conversation.

"Tell me, girl, is RJ gonna chew your ass for this little excursion?"

"There's no doubt about it," she sighed, "But you know what? I just don't care."

"That's my girl."

"Sometimes," she continued, "I wish everything was different. I walk out in the yard and see pelicans fly by and monkeys swinging in the trees."

"These rednecks around here would start hunting them. You'd see King Kong's head hanging beside King Louie's above my mantle."

"If you really want a challenging sport, you should try to snag virgins," she flirted.

"Are you a virgin?" he asked. Amber hung her head and blushed. "I'm sorry, Amber. That was an inappropriate question."

"Hey, I brought it up," she confessed, "Besides, it's okay. I'm not a virgin."

Amber lied to him. The truth was, she did not know the condition of her purity. She understood a lot about sex and felt comfortable with sexual situations. Yet she could not remember ever doing it. If she was a virgin, she figured that would come to an end before the next sunrise.

They enjoyed dinner in Lexington. She never imagined Kurt liked Chinese food. Love is built with tiny bricks. Little things brought them closer together; the snowball she threw at him outside the restaurant and Kurt's tone deaf sing-a-long with a George Strait song on the radio. As the sky donned its evening gown, they made their way to the club. There, little things delivered large impact.

Her movements flashed like still frames in his mind. Dance floor lights splashed red across the wall. She fashioned her hair in perfect chaos. It wasn't pinned evenly, yet somehow looked beautiful and wild. One long strand of bangs draped on each side of her face. A slight smile, just wide enough to curve her cheeks, kept perfect position on full, ruby lips. Her eyes held a curious expression, looking Kurt over. Not a blemish could be found on Amber's creamy skin. She looked young and undeniably perfect, splitting the smoke and shattering the red.

Then she sat across from him and gently brushed a strand of bangs away from her face. The smile widened but her lips closed.

Eyes retreated from wide curiosity to glimmering slivers, flirtatiously devouring every calorie of Kurt's attention. A soft song with a strong beat charmed a hundred snakes' hearts. Their bodies weaved with the melody's seduction.

Her essence redefined everything Kurt knew of love and desire. He spent seven years married to a woman. Surely they shared intimate moments that seemed powerful at the time. That power, however, wilted with Amber's presence. Love Kurt felt before that night became merely a fluke- a joke- meaningless and inferior. Nothing cleanses a man's heart of a woman more than another woman. In an instant, he pictured a thousand days with Amber.

(Mornings, brazenly gold, when he wakes to lemon slices of sunshine beaming through creases in the bedroom curtains; she sits at the foot of the bed, tenderly rubbing his leg, her hair hanging in a ponytail on the side. Her face is a mixture of bright white and silky caramel, illuminated here and shaded there by sunlight. Timidly, she slants her right shoulder upward and rests her head on the arch. No words are spoken. A simple, silent connection welcomes the first day of forever.

Afternoons with her hair down, a lusty look from over her shoulder. Evenings on the town dressed in black, her entire face a smile, arms loosely wrapping his waist.)

He saw her a thousand different ways and all of them were beautiful. To Amber, Kurt was unreal; safety, happiness, and excitement rolled into the frame of a man. He made her feel gorgeous.

Kurt proved his point. He was the worst dancer in the whole joint. Yet Amber felt proud in his arms. They laughed and danced. Hours melted like snow. It was Amber who suggested they stay the night in Lexington, where they at least had electricity. Kurt could not refuse.

There they were in the honeymoon suite, courtesy of Amber Rockhouse's credit card. Electricity had been the excuse, but passion was the lure. They only spent about ten minutes with the lights on. As he roamed her body, and the heat neared climax, a thought flashed for merely a split second in Amber's mind. She saw herself falling from a rock cliff, arms and legs flailing, ground racing toward her face. It was the closest thing she ever had to a pre-Rockhouse memory. Excitement gripped her, and she melted in his arms. A door had been opened, a secret passage discovered. There could be no doubt in either of their minds that what they made, beneath satin sheets of a Lexington honeymoon suite, was love.

Third Quarter
Merry-Go-Round
1.

Arthur met Judith in a rundown, honky-tonk bar. He figured she must have been about eighteen, and he was right. She should have never been allowed through the door, but girls like Judith get a lot of favors just by being alive. Arthur thought, "What the hell? Might as well roll the dice."

"So, I guess this is where I'm supposed to have something clever to say," Arthur sneered, as he slid beside her at the bar.

"How's about you just give me a cigarette and I'll dance with you?" Judith replied.

"Are you old enough to smoke?"

"I'm old enough to do a lot of things."

"You're not old enough to be in this bar."

"Then why am I here?"

As they danced, the magnetism was undeniable. They held each other tight, but relaxed, swaying to the music. Arthur's fingers gently stroked the back of Judith's neck. She smiled and tilted her caramel head backwards, giving him more room to roam.

"I guess I should know your name," Judith smirked.

"It's Arthur, but you can call me baby."

"Okay, Arthur Baby. I'm Judith."

She was a cute little thing. Caramel hair twisted across her nougat neck and softly coated cinnamon shoulders. Her body curved like Venus sculpted of candy. Judith liked Arthur right away. He was a good looking boy- round apple bottom, baby blue eyes, and sandy hair sitting high and tight above chiseled cheekbones. At age twenty-eight, he satisfied Judith's taste for older men. With his white t-shirt tucked tightly into faded jeans, he looked like something Judith had only seen on a movie screen.

Situations like this usually lead to one night. Once in a lucky while, they render more. Neither of them had anything to lose. Arthur lived with his brother, Jerry. Judith lived wherever. They capitalized on every chance to make love. However, the conversations they shared those first few nights together were what truly sparked a devoted relationship. A small community park sat across the street from Jerry's house. Their second night together, midnight found Arthur and Judith alone in the park, cuddling each other on the merry-go-round.

"Tell me about yourself," Judith requested, with her head resting on his shoulder.

"Well, my mom and dad are dead."

"Oh my goodness," she gasped, "what happened?"

"Heart attack with dad. Cancer with mom."

"How old were they?"

"In their sixties. They got started having kids late."

"I'm sorry to hear that you don't have them."

"Jerry is cool. We get along good. He's the only family I've got."

"I'm adopted," she groaned, "My real mom's name is Brenda. She's a major league ho. Chelsea adopted me. She's Brenda's sister. So, my mom is my aunt. I bet that makes you wanna hop in the sack with me, don't it?"

"You have something in common with Jesus, Moses, and Superman."

"What's that?"

"All of you were adopted."

The merry-go-round became their Terabithia; secrets shared beneath spinning stars. Through all the hours spent satisfying lust in the bedroom or backseat of Arthur's car, it was simple declarations on a twirling metal platform that cemented love.

"You know, I'm not perfect," Arthur admitted, leaning against the rusty merry-go-round bars.

"Nobody is, Arthur Baby," Judith replied, sprawled out on the platform's center, "except me."

"I think you should know that I have an addiction, a bad one."

"Are you a junky?" she asked, sitting up.

"No," he answered, staring at the moon, "not anymore."

"Well, the past is the past, Arthur. I don't even want to talk about the stuff I've done. I was pretty young when I got started."

"My addiction destroyed my life. I'll always be a slave to it. I've put all of that behind me, but it still eats at me, and I just thought you should know."

"Maybe a good woman can straighten you out."

"A good woman is the only thing that can straighten me out."

And that is exactly what Judith did. She never asked about his addiction, and he offered no further information. The past remained buried in silence. Arthur's cravings went away for awhile. But he knew, eventually actions would disclose the secret he could not reveal with words. Some mornings, he watched Judith sleep, hoping, with tears in his eyes, that he would never hurt her. Then came the day Arthur arrived home from work about an hour late. He sounded like a blind bull barreling through the kitchen. Judith arose from bed. With all the banging and thumping, she was afraid that Arthur was engaged in a fight with a burglar.

She snatched her glasses off the end table, shedding a cocoon of blankets and batting sleep from heavy eyelids in the trailer's shivering cold. Groggy and off-balance, she tiptoed down the hall, halfway expecting to confront an intruder. Arthur stood with his back to Judith at the kitchen sink, splashing water on his face. A couple of dishes were shattered on the floor. Pots and pans scattered as far as the hallway.

"Is everything okay, Arthur?"

"Go back to bed, Judith," he growled.

"Baby, what's wrong?"

Arthur turned toward her. His face, hands, and sweatshirt were soaked with blood.

"Oh my God," Judith shrieked.

"I told you to go back to bed," he snarled.

Crazy, gray eyes pierced through Judith. His pupils were nearly round as dimes. Rapidly, Arthur's jugular swelled and shrank like a muscle. Veins on his forehead followed suit, pulsating with angry rhythm. He snarled to the point of drooling. Blood dripped from his chin and smeared across his face, as thick as makeup. Maternal instinct kicked in and Judith hurried across the kitchen to doctor his wounds.

"You're hurt," she panicked.

"No," he shouted, "you should go away!"

"What did I do?"

"You woke up!"

Arthur pushed her out of the way with enough force to hurt. He then picked up one of the cooking pots and hurled it through the hallway. Judith's shattered feelings showed in her eyes.

"Oh my God," she gasped, "you're high!"

"I am crazy," he declared, screaming at her with a beastly roar, "an insane manifestation, a freak of nature, I am no good!"

"Calm down, baby," she pleaded, moving to the opposite side of the kitchen table to prevent him from grabbing hold of her, "Listen, if you caved in and got high, it's okay, just calm down."

Panting for breath, he stared incoherently in all directions, with his head bobbing like a chicken. Every gurgling exhale sent drops of blood spraying from his lips. Arthur's tongue clicked like an egg timer inside his mouth. For about fifteen seconds he peered across the room, staring right through Judith, as if she wasn't there. Then he suddenly took off, almost jogging.

"I've got a Beatles c.d. somewhere," he ranted, charging through the hall.

"Okay," she whined, with heavy concern for his well being.

"Where the hell is it?" he shouted.

"I don't know," she panicked, "but the electricity is still off, so you can't listen to it right now."

She heard him in the bedroom ripping drawers all the way out of the dresser. That is when her fear transformed to anger. Judith burst into the bedroom, nearly sprinting. Arthur continued blindly chucking everything he got his hands on. She scanned the room, looking for something to hit him with. The only thing she could find was her vibrator, tucked in an underwear drawer Arthur slung on the bed. She gripped the vibrator and proceeded to thump Arthur upside the head with it, hard enough to thud against his skull.

"What the hell is wrong with you?" she screamed with every thud, "Stop it! I don't know if you are hurt or high or what the hell is going on, but you better get a grip or I'm gonna beat you to death with this vibrator, Arthur!"

He pushed Judith down on the bed. She hit her head on the underwear drawer so hard it made her cry.

"Can't you see I'm covered in blood?" he snarled, holding her down.

"You're scaring me," she sobbed.

Arthur turned her loose and backed away from the bed. For a

moment, he swayed side to side and Judith feared he was going to pass out on the bedroom floor. With his fingertips, he softly massaged pulsing veins on his forehead.

"I want my Beatles c.d.," he said, calmly, as if nothing out of the ordinary had occurred.

"Jesus, Arthur," Judith cried, "If it means that much to you, I'll go into town and buy you a damn Beatles c.d. Hell, I'll buy their whole freakin' catalogue."

"What do you know about music?" he scoffed, "All you ever listen to is that hokey ass country shit."

"Oh yeah," she angrily laughed, rising from the bed, adjusting her glasses, and clutching her vibrator, "Well, the Beatles are fags, Arthur. That's what you like. You like faggots."

He nodded, with his mouth drooped open like an imbecile. A few short grunts rolled out of his throat, and he wagged his head, sending drops of blood splattering across the sheet.

"I think I better leave," he stated, turning toward the hall.

"Don't bother," she barked, charging past him, "I'll leave."

Judith picked a pair of sweatpants from their pile of dirty laundry and fumbled, slipping them over her legs. She didn't even realize they were on backwards. Arthur followed her into the living room and tumbled across the couch, as she stuffed her purse full of bare necessities.

"I'm going to Shirley's," she sobbed, "I'll be back for my stuff later."

Judith didn't wait for a response. She slammed the door, leaving him sprawled on the couch. Now, the trailer and relationship were a mess, thanks to Arthur.

As he slouched on the sofa, the kitchen light popped to life. Electricity had been restored. Arthur did not turn on the television or rush to take a shower. Instead, he sat in dim silence throughout the morning, reflecting on the horrible mistake he made. He realized he could not keep lying to Judith. Yet he did not know how to tell her that the blood, soaking his sweatshirt and covering her hands, was not his.

2.

After nearly a week of dark silence, town glowed and hummed at midnight like a tiny Las Vegas. Sidewalks and streets were empty. In fact, most folks crawled into bed early to enjoy the first warm sleep they had in days. Yet town seemed alive. Porch lights burned. Heating units purred. Windows looked like blinking eyes with the flicker of television screens. In Sugarland, every trailer boasted an illuminated window, except for lot #1. With Arthur and Judith gone, their windows told the story of darkness inside the home.

Even in hollows on the outskirts of town, night regained a pulse. All roads within city limits, as well as major arteries leading out of the county, were clear and relatively safe. But the blizzard was far from a memory. Town always received emergency attention first. In outer parts of the county, thousands remained without power and heat.

Traffic accidents, on icy mountain roads, kept emergency crews in route 24/7. Temperatures refused to rise above freezing. Weather reports indicated that it would be awhile before the sun devoted enough energy to melt ice and snow. Accumulation totals were not the worst ever recorded. Overall, twelve to fifteen inches of snow blanketed the area. Thus far, no one died as a result of the blizzard. But with each day, the mood grew more anxious. People had to work. Yet driving to work meant possible death.

In town, however, folks felt as if the tribulation was nearly over. They cheered the functions of electrical appliances, usually taken for granted, and slept peacefully in the soft glow of television light, as heating vents spewed conditioned comfort.

Even poor, ol' Kurt managed to sneak in a few winks. The blizzard had, perhaps, been roughest for him. On top of the demands his job presented during times of crisis, he had worry for EJ and excitement for Amber limiting precious sleep-time. The recommended eight hours of slumber seemed laughable to

Kurt. He was lucky to get eight hours in two nights. Something always interrupted his dreams; usually one of the deputies requesting assistance at a crime scene, or a concerned citizen, who believes her vote is worth a phone call to the sheriff at five in the morning to report a stolen dog. Other times the blame fell on paperwork, stress, or simply a late night movie. Whatever the reason, there was no sleep for the sheriff. But on the night electricity returned, the phone surprisingly stayed silent. His job's demands, brother's stupidity, and girlfriend's breasts were unable to distract him from a deep doze. The only thing that could sever his bliss would be an intruder fumbling through the house.

In all his time as a law enforcer, no one ever broke into Kurt's home or showed up on the doorstep in a fit of rage. Still, he practiced caution. A good sheriff makes lots of enemies. Normally, he bolted the house solid at bedtime. During the power outage, however, Kurt left the front door unlocked, out of concern that EJ might have lost his keys. He installed a battery operated buzzer on the door, sort of as a safety net. With Kurt sleeping on the couch in the living room, if the door opened in the middle of the night, the buzzer would easily wake him. Once electricity came back on, Kurt craved the comfort of his bed. Out of habit, he did not lock the front door.

Rooms made of wood have great acoustics. Under typical circumstances, the buzzer would wake Kurt, even in the bedroom. But when the acoustics are occupied by the sounds of Sports Center on the bedroom television, a rickety ceiling fan spinning at top speed, and a central heating unit laboring to catch up on a week's worth of work... a cheap buzzer will not act as a sufficient alarm.

Kurt slept soundly, while someone entered the house, activated the buzzer, and stumbled over boots he left on a place mat, blurting out curse words the entire time. The intruder shuffled into the kitchen and scavenged through cabinets, until finding a can of coffee. The faucet spewed water into the coffee pot and percolation began. Every other step on Kurt's stairway creaked, but he did not hear. In fact, the intruder could have showered, vacuumed, and hosted a party. Kurt would have never known. Yet something gentle finally woke him. The intruder sat on his mattress. That soft shifting of weight brought Kurt into consciousness. His eyes popped wide open with the vision of a silhouette. "Is this a robber, a ghost, an angel?" he thought, "No... it's Amber."

"Amber, what are you doing here?"

He turned on the bedside lamp. Amber trembled violently; her lips blue, cheeks pink, and tears flowing.

"I'm sorry. I just needed to see you really bad."

"It's okay," he groaned, rising onto an elbow, "I'm glad to see you. How did you get here?"

"I walked."

"Walked? My God, it's in the twenties out there."

"I'm okay. I bundled up good."

"Why didn't you call me?"

"I needed to walk. I'm having some problems, Kurt. I almost killed myself tonight. The only thing that kept me from doing it is you."

"Amber, baby, what's wrong?"

Removing her turquoise toboggan, sweaty hair spilled into lime eyes. Moisture deepened her hair's tone from strawberry to near purple; a crown of fire, flickering wildly- uncombed, untamed, yet wickedly beautiful. One eye peeped from the flame, tears streaming. She looked like a brokenhearted kid- lost and hungry- yearning for comfort yet burning with angst, as her overcoat and scarf slithered to the floor. Teardrops soaked the collar of her lavender sweater. Kurt thought she might rip right out of her skin.

"I was going to jump from my balcony," she sobbed, "I had one foot on the rail. But all I could think about was you. I wanted to see you so bad. I'm sorry."

"No, no," he comforted, "everything is fine. Let's go downstairs and talk about this over some coffee."

"I already made coffee for you," she sniffled, "I knew you would want some."

Kurt helped Amber from the bed. Her eyes tilted upward, staring straight into his. A powerful burst of passion spontaneously consumed him. All he could think about was lifting her until their lips came together in a lust crazed kiss, as they fell to the mattress, ripping each others clothes off. Somehow, Kurt curbed the urge. He knew that was not what she needed. For crying out loud, she nearly committed suicide only hours earlier, and then walked about four miles through the frigid darkness.

Truthfully, he did not know exactly what Amber needed... a lover, a savior, someone to talk to? But for a brief second, she stood silently within his embrace; quivering lips close enough for him to feel her breath. She did nothing but stare deep into his eyes. Was she contemplating or perhaps anticipating? Amber made it impossible for him to think straight. He needed a blindfold. Looking at her was hard to do because she looked so good.

"Come on," he persuaded, "I need a strong drink."

Hand in hand, they walked downstairs. It was a peaceful morning, about four o'clock. Kurt flipped lights on along the way. Amber could almost feel the house groan as it awoke. Even the mountains appeared to be sleeping through the living room window. In the kitchen, he helped her into a chair at the table and poured each of them a cup of coffee.

"Suicide?" he calmly lectured, taking a seat across from her, "Seriously, Amber, what was you thinking?"

"I'm miserable, Kurt. I didn't know how miserable I was until you made me happy. I really care about you."

"Well, I care about you too, honey."

Amber struggled to steady the mug. Hot coffee dribbled down her chin. She didn't seem to notice.

"I have to tell you the truth," she sighed, "If you don't want to be with me anymore after you hear this, I understand. But will you please hear me out?"

"Sure."

Amber leaned forward like she was about to reveal a great secret. Her face immediately flushed pale. For a few seconds the only sound was the refrigerator's hum. Amber bit her quivering lip and tightly closed her eyes. Obviously, she feared this secret would forever change destiny. With eyes still closed and hands clutched into fists on the tabletop, she whispered.

"I'm a zombie."

Kurt placed his hands over her fists and softly massaged. She opened her eyes, freeing a solitary tear. Tenderly, his thumb brushed the tear away. Amber did not expect such a sincere reaction.

"I know you need some rest, baby," he comforted, "You've got to get out of that mansion."

He misunderstood her to be speaking metaphorically.

"Kurt, you don't understand. I am a zombie... for real. You

know... the living dead."

He leaned back, away from her, like she had some kind of contagious disease. The expression on his face appeared more confused than frightened. Kurt glanced at Amber, took a sip of coffee, then stared at the floor in deep thought. At least he didn't laugh at her, which was what she expected.

"Aren't zombies drooling imbeciles that eat brains?" he asked, non-sarcastically.

"In some movies they are," she answered, "and there are some like that in real life. But a zombie is simply someone who was once dead, but now is alive."

"I don't understand."

"RJ Rockhouse is a necromancer. Do you know what that means?"

"No."

"A necromancer is a sorcerer, who can invoke spirits of the dead. He can talk to them, make them appear, and in advanced cases like RJ's, he can bring a spirit back to life by placing it in a dead body."

"Okay."

She nervously tugged at her hair then ran fingernails down the length of her face, like she was itching to claw her eyes out. With the exception of slight trembling, she managed to keep her voice calm.

"When I was a teenager... I mean, when my body was a teenager, I fell off a cliff in the woods back behind RJ's mansion. He just so happened to find me there. I was still alive, but died not long after he found me. RJ placed a spirit in my body and brought it back to life."

Kurt's surprise wore off and gave way to agitation.

"Amber, listen to what you are saying."

"I know you think I'm crazy."

"No, that's not it at all. I think you honestly believe what you're telling me. I also think you are the victim of an insane, overly possessive old man."

"Kurt, I have seen things you cannot believe."

"You've got to get away from that mansion right now. And we need to get you some help."

She stood and paced the table's length, back and forth, with one hand on her hip and the other holding her forehead.

"Therapy isn't going to fix it, Kurt," she whined, "I am the combination of a spirit and body that do not belong here."

"Amber, you've got to understand why this is hard for me to accept."

The kitchen wallpaper's print was of large rosebushes in bloom, reminiscent of the Victorian-Era. Amber stood with her back to the wall. A white mist seemed to surround her. She was a divine vision, rising from the roses on a cottony cloud, like a seductive spirit- a forbidden fruit- a venomous serpent singing a hypnotic song. Her face was so pretty and vulnerable, Kurt wanted to scoop her tiny, trembling body into his strong arms and kiss the sadness away. Yet her eyes held a sinister deadness- a lack of conscience- like a meat-eating flower luring its prey near with colorful petals and sweet smelling nectar.

"I do understand, Kurt. This is hard for me, too. I know you will dump me after you hear this. But I have never told anyone these things. So, please, just hear me out."

"I am, baby."

"I can't remember anything before the fall. I don't know what my name was or where I came from."

"Hold it right there," Kurt commanded, "Something isn't right with this story. This is a small county, Amber. If a teenage girl goes missing, everybody knows about it."

"I know what you're thinking," she said, returning to the chair, "It's strange that no one came looking for me. I've thought about that myself."

"Don't you think it's possible that Rockhouse had you kidnapped?"

"Why would he do that?"

"So he can practice his freaky voodoo. I bet that's it. He had you kidnapped then brainwashed you."

"It doesn't really matter if he found me in the woods or kidnapped me. I'm still a zombie."

Kurt refilled their mugs and sat at the table, sipping coffee with no reply. His silence troubled Amber. When it came to sensitive issues, she felt as if "Kurt the Sheriff" overpowered "Kurt the Man". It seemed like he was always trying to find a crime in every problem.

"RJ is a necromancer, Kurt. You can question what I know about where I came from, but you cannot question what I know about RJ's necromancy. I live there. I see it. If he kidnapped me, he did it to practice necromancy. So, regardless of what happened when I was a teenager, I am a zombie now."

"Amber, if he's out there kidnapping young girls, don't you think he needs to be stopped?"

Amber slammed her fists on the table, startling Kurt so bad, he spilled hot coffee all over his naked chest. Leveraging on her fists, she rose from the chair. Her face turned cherry red.

"You don't even care about me," she growled, "All you care about is arresting somebody!"

"What are you talking about?"

Amber dropped back into the chair, crying again. Kurt's face was a dumbfounded mess.

"I can't trust you," she fumed.

"Why do you say that?"

"To the best of my knowledge, he's never kidnapped anybody. And to tell you the truth, I don't think he kidnapped me."

"Okay, just calm down, Amber."

"I don't want you going up there to arrest him, Kurt. That's not why I'm here, and that's not what I need from you."

"Jesus, Amber, I don't think you have anything to worry about. What am I going to do, arrest him on the charge of abusing zombies?"

"Don't make fun of me, Kurt! You can go to Hell!"

Suddenly, Kurt became ashamed of himself. Amber's sadness pushed her to the brink of suicide. The one thing that gave her hope was him. So, she walked through a blizzard's aftermath simply to be by his side. The contents of her heart lay at his feet for him to lovingly cradle or cruelly trample. He had no problem nurturing her needs in the bedroom. However, real men are nurturers at the kitchen table as easily as they are between the sheets, and Kurt knew that.

"I'm sorry," he admitted, "You don't need me to solve your problems. You just need me to listen. Well, that's what I'll do, baby. Say whatever you need to say and I'll be here as your friend, okay?"

Amber's emotions changed with the quickness of a water faucet shifting from hot to cold. Within the time it takes to swallow a gulp of coffee, she transformed from cherry red anger to the peach bliss of a young girl lost in love.

"Do you like me?" she timidly asked.

"A little too much," he confessed.

"Do I freak you out?"

"A little too much," he grinned.

Amber laughed.

"The reason I wanted you to know all of this is because I really like you, Kurt. You are wonderful."

"Thank you, sweetie."

"The thought of being your girlfriend makes me so happy, and I have never been happy. But I can't be unfair to you, baby, even if it costs me the only happiness I've ever known."

"What makes you think you're being unfair?"

"Not telling you about the clock would be really unfair to you... the most unfair thing ever."

"What clock?"

Amber reached across the table to hold Kurt's hands. He had never seen a woman transition from bitter to sweet so quickly. One second she was a wrathful demon... next second, the purest of angels.

"There is a rule in necromancy," she instructed, "RJ calls it 'the clock law'. A zombie is like a clock, and the necromancer is the battery. As long as the battery is good, the clock will continue ticking. But when the battery dies, the clock dies, too. That means I will die when RJ does, and he is about to turn a hundred."

Amber released his hands and waited for a response. Kurt offered none. Instead, he crossed his arms and stared at the tabletop, lost in thought.

"I can't flirt with you and try to make you like me without letting you know that I'm a short timer," she continued, "but will you promise me something? If you don't want to be in a relationship with me, I understand. But please don't abandon me. I need someone to talk to. Promise me you won't leave me all alone, without a friend."

Kurt walked around the table to her side.

"Come here," he invited.

Amber stood and he embraced her tightly.

"I won't abandon you," he promised, "I'll be right by your side whenever you need me. But you have to promise me two things. No more of this suicide nonsense. If something else kills you, so be it, but if you're going to kill yourself, I want nothing to do with you. And you've got to move in here with me. I want you out of that mansion. This is your home now. Will you promise me those two things?"

Amber bounced up and down, cheering like a child on Christmas morning.

"Do you mean it, Kurt? Do you really, really mean it?"

"Yes," he laughed.

"I promise," she swore, smiling joyfully, "no suicide. And I will come live here with you, my baby!"

She danced through the house like a freed fugitive. Her jubilant cries woke the outside world. Kurt sat at the table thinking, "What the hell am I doing?" He did not believe her to be a zombie. However, he did realize Amber's deep emotional troubles and the possible problems asking her to move in could pose. But Kurt also knew that it was useless for him to try and resist her. The day they met, he thought it foolish for them to go out and play pool in a blizzard, but he went anyway. He considered it unwise to call her for a second date. Two days later they were cheek to cheek in a Lexington nightclub. Kurt's better judgment told him not to stay overnight with her in Lexington. Sure enough, the following morning dawned, with them snuggled naked in a hotel bed. Now, Kurt faced another decision concerning Amber. The logical answer was obvious. Once again, the sheriff willingly turned his back on logic. He couldn't figure out what kind of power she had over his reasoning.

"Hey, baby," Amber chirped, stepping into the kitchen doorway, wearing only her bra and panties, "I was just wondering if you wanted to come to bed."

3.

Judith stared at the playground through Shirley's living room window. An icy merry-go-round glistened in streetlight. Although frozen see-saws held perfectly still, she imagined them rising and falling at steady pace, like her emotions. Shirley was a great friend, and her home offered a peaceful, cheery atmosphere. Judith laughed at Shirley's jokes and danced with little Brandon to pop music booming on the stereo. But sadness underscored Judith's smiles. Two days passed since her argument with Arthur. She had not seen or spoken to him. Their separation happened so suddenly and without explanation, Judith could not comprehend. Anger melted but confusion remained. She just wanted to talk to him and try to figure out what the hell went wrong.

Judith regularly stepped out for a cigarette, even though Shirley allowed smoking in the trailer. Lot #1 could not be seen from lot #6. She must have gone through two packs of smokes, slipping over to the center of Sugarland, peeking to see if Arthur's car sat in their driveway. Each cigarette brought disappointment.

Her intuition suggested that Arthur had a moment of weakness. Perhaps an old drug buddy came into the store, offering a cheap (or possibly even free) high. Arthur caved in. Afterwards, he fell down, walked into something, or got into a fight. Whatever the reason for his bloody face might have been, she figured Arthur was high and felt guilty. Judith justified their turmoil with intuitive conclusions, but truthfully, she didn't know what happened.

At least she had Shirley. Without her new friend, the situation could have been critical. Shirley's son was a cutie. He lit up the cold evening like only a four year old can. Judith danced with Brandon until her feet hurt. No matter how many times she twirled him into a dip, he always wanted "more, more, more".

Shirley's brother, Arnold, hung out with them that night. Arnold lived in the southern end of the county. Electricity had not been restored there. He was a nice, laid back boy. Regardless of what played on the TV or radio, Arnold seemed to enjoy it. He simply appreciated relaxing in a place where the temperature stayed above fifty degrees and one could walk to the bathroom without worrying about shattering a shin bone on furniture in the dark.

"Brandon, baby, you've got to give Judith a break," Shirley lectured, "She's an old woman, not a young stud like you."

"I want dip! I want dip!" he cheered.

"It's okay," Judith panted, "I'm finally spending an evening with a man who knows how to have a good time."

If ever a child pageant winner existed, Brandon was the one. Long, curly locks of gold bounced as he danced. His blue eyes were bright as August sky and round as silver dollars. The perfect amount of baby fat dangled on his cheeks to inspire a firm pinch. To top it all off, Shirley dressed him in bibbed overalls. Judith didn't really want children, but she had no problem hanging out with that one.

"I tell you what," Shirley negotiated, "how's about mommy dancing with you a little while to give Judith a break? Then she can dance one more song with you before bedtime."

"I want dip! I want dip!" he demanded, spilling giggles that made them all forget it was winter.

"Mommy will dip you," Shirley promised.

The song changed, as Brandon took her by the hand.

"Just my luck," she groaned, "another fast one."

Arnold finally spoke. He was a man of few words, but when he did say something, it usually sparked laughter.

"Hold on a minute," he exclaimed, rising from the couch, "that's one of my favorite songs, 'Hungry Like the Wolf' by Duran, Duran. I think uncle Arnold is gonna cut in on this one."

Arnold began shimmying across the living room floor. Judith cackled so hard she nearly wet herself. She couldn't believe he was Shirley's brother. They looked nothing alike. Shirley had the appearance of a model with her mocha brown hair and crystal blue eyes. Arnold was by no means handsome. He looked like the typical man in their native town, wearing a blue Kentucky Wildcats baseball cap that did not match his black and red AC/DC t-shirt. Blue jeans, a size too small, snuggled chicken legs. Every second passed with a cigarette either dangling from his lips or pinched between his fingers. He had the kind of stubble beard that not even sandpaper could erase. But Arnold was impossible to dislike, especially when his bony butt wiggled emphatically to Duran, Duran.

"I'm on the hunt. I'm after you," he sang, "and I'm hungry like the wolf."

Whenever the line "hungry like the wolf" rolled around, Arnold howled at the ceiling and tapped his foot. Brandon mimicked him.

"Oh my God," Judith wheezed, still laughing, "you all have killed me. I've got to step outside for a smoke."

"Now, Judith," Shirley teased, "you're either gonna have to start smoking in here or tell us the real reason you're going outside every ten minutes."

"I'm just restless," Judith whined.

"Mmm hmm," Shirley smiled, "you're curious is what it is. You're afraid he's gonna come home and get gone again without you knowing about it."

"I'm just restless, Shirley, and I feel better when I go outside."

"I want outside! I want outside!" Brandon whaled in mid-shuffle.

"Honey, you know what's best for you," Shirley comforted, "If you want to go home, that's your call, baby doll. But you're more than welcome to stay here."

"Thank you, Shirley. I want to stay here, even if he does come home tonight. But walking outside makes me feel better. I'm just restless; that's all."

"I want outside! I want outside!" Brandon shrieked.

"Oh no," mommy replied, "it's getting late, Brandon, and it's really cold outside."

"Maybe that would make me feel better," Judith said, "if you all took a walk with me, just to the playground and back. I mean, I know it's cold outside and everything, but that would probably cheer me up."

"Okay," Shirley surrendered, flashing a wink at Brandon, "but we've got to bundle you up good if you're gonna take a walk, my boy."

"Yippee!" he howled, already on his way to the closet.

"You're going too, Arnold," Judith commanded.

"Why not," he snickered, "If I can handle a week in a trailer with icicles hanging off the ceiling, I reckon I can handle a walk to the playground and back."

One week earlier, the monkey bars and swing-sets were all that could be detected on Sugarland's playground. Everything else blended into one dimensional white beneath a coating of snow. With school cancelled and parents home from work, children gathered on the playground during afternoon hours, despite cold temperatures. Winter boots beat most of the snow into muddy sludge. Unblemished precipitation, remaining on the ground, felt as if its texture was weakening. Judith remembered making a snowball, one day after the blizzard passed. That snowball held firm like concrete, heavy and hard in her hands. Now, attempts to pack snow only resulted in a sleeve soaking gush of water. Maybe the winter would eventually come to an end, after all.

Brandon's cuteness continued, even when covered from head to toe. The snowsuit prevented his arms from bending. They jutted straight out on both sides like the arms of a starfish. Every sentence started with "I want", but he was so damn adorable, everybody came as close as they possibly could to fulfilling all of his childish desires.

Judith wore a red hoodie, zipped all the way up to her chin. Shirley strutted her stuff in a black leather jacket. Arnold, of course, didn't give a flying rat's fanny about the cold. He walked against frigid wind, showing no discomfort, like his AC/DC t-shirt was made of polar bear pelts.

All other children in Sugarland were asleep. But Brandon, being too young for school and having a nocturnal mother, skipped toward the playground, as if frolicking in noon sunshine.

"I look up to you, Shirley," Judith confessed.

"Why would you ever look up to me?"

"You've got it all figured out."

"What do you think I have figured out?"

"Life… You're doing good and you're happy."

"Well," Shirley sighed, eyes smiling as she watched Brandon skip, "that little boy is my everything. He keeps my life straight."

"I'm serious," Judith reiterated, "You always know what needs to be done. I don't have any idea what to do with my situation."

"Do you love Arthur?"

"Yes," Judith confirmed, "I've never really been in love before, but I know I love Arthur. I just can't figure out what's going on with him; that's all."

"Judith, I don't think women are supposed to be able to figure men out. That's just nature's way. If I had figured Brandon's daddy out, there's no way I would have got fixed up with him. Then I never would have had my precious little boy. So, as bad as it sucks sometimes, it's probably best if we never understand men."

"I thought I had everything with Arthur figured out until the other day. Now, I really don't know what to do."

"Judith, honey, my experiences with men have all been bad. So, I would probably tell you to enjoy a man during the honeymoon phase and kick him to the curb, when that phase is over. But you love Arthur. So, I guess you've got to figure out if the other day was just a one time thing or if it is something you can expect out of him on a day to day basis. If it's a one time thing, forgive him and move on. If he does it again, get the hell away from him and stay gone."

Brandon stopped skipping and waddled from side to side, spinning as best he could without the ability of bending knees. Once he faced Shirley, skipping began again, this time at a more rapid pace. Ice crunched, as Brandon teetered left to right like a penguin on speed. Finally, he reached mommy. Tiny mittens tugged the hem of her jacket. Chubby cheeks glowed scarlet and watery eyes projected concern.

"Mommy," he whispered.

"Yes, baby."

"I gotta pee."

Judith found his plea hilarious. Shirley, however, wasn't laughing.

"Brandon," she barked, "are you serious? Why didn't you pee before we left the house?"

"I don't know," he whimpered, "I gotta pee."

"My God," Shirley grumbled, "If I don't take him now, he'll pee all in his snowsuit."

"Mommy, can I pee out here?"

"No, Brandon, somebody might see you, and you've got all those clothes on. I can't get you undressed and then dressed again out here. Come on, I'll take you to the house."

Poor Brandon... his little lip began to quiver and tears swelled in his eyes. Shirley grabbed him by a mitten and stomped toward home.

"You all go ahead," she huffed, "It'll take me a few minutes to get him out of this snowsuit and back in it again, but we'll catch up with you as soon as he's finished."

They hurried away, Shirley cussing the entire time, with Brandon slipping in an "I want" at every possible opportunity. Judith turned to Arnold and smiled. Until that moment, she forgot he was walking with them.

"Arnold, you don't talk much."

"I talk," he defended, non-excitedly, "If a man goes ten seconds without talking, a woman thinks there's something wrong with him."

"Talking makes the time pass quicker. It keeps you from getting bored."

"A man, who doesn't know when to close his mouth, can talk himself into some foolish things."

Judith didn't respond. She simply stuffed her hands in the hoodie's kangaroo pocket and walked on in silence. Nothing made even the slightest squeak. It seemed a giant vacuum had somehow swallowed Sugarland. Judith considered screaming at the top of her lungs just to shatter the unsettling hush. Arnold's social graces left a lot to be desired. Yet she wasn't frustrated with him. He knew how to serve up a good laugh when desperately needed. Besides, he was right. People continuously told Judith she talked too much.

It did not take them long to reach the playground. Arnold stopped at the blacktop's edge and lit a cigarette. Judith kept right on marching through the mud, sinking up to her ankles in some places. The expression on her face revealed childlike fascination, as she studied every structure.

"I love playgrounds," she marveled, "but there's something I can't figure out."

"What's that?" Arnold mumbled, watching her from the parking lot like a babysitter.

"I can't figure out if empty playgrounds in the middle of the night are peaceful or creepy."

"It ain't creepy," he shivered, "It's cold."

Judith hummed a happy tune, giving each bar on the merry-go-round a swift tap as it twirled. She removed her red hood and, every few seconds, looked over at Arnold, with a smile. Judith slightly flirted, not because she found him attractive or intended to do anything physical. She was bored and wanted to see if Arnold even realized when a girl flirted with him. So far, he did not. She swayed to the front of the merry-go-round and stopped it from spinning. Continuing to sneak occasional glances at Arnold, Judith used her finger to doodle squiggly lines in moisture on the aluminum bars.

"Did you ever play on the playground when you was little?" she asked timidly.

"I reckon everybody played on the playground when they was little," he said, barely above a mumble. Judith couldn't tell if he was lighting one cigarette after another or simply taking a very long time to smoke the first one.

"What was your favorite thing on the playground?" she queried.

"I liked to swing," he answered quickly, with no deliberation.

"Swings don't count," she declared, "Everybody likes to swing. What was your favorite thing other than the swings?"

"I don't know. I just bounced around from one thing to another."

"My favorite is the merry-go-round," she boasted, "I love it, love it, love it! Why don't you come over here and take a spin?"

"I hate the merry-go-round," he grumbled, "All that spinning makes me puke."

"Arnold, you're about as fun as the clap," she teased, sitting on the icy platform.

Finally, he dropped his cigarette and treaded through mud until he was by Judith's side.

"I reckon you're needin' somebody to talk to," he noted, "Are you havin' troubles with your man?"

"I guess so," she groaned, "I haven't talked to him in two days."

Arnold sat on the cold platform and lit another cigarette, staring at the clear, midnight sky.

"Y'all ain't married," he said, "and you don't have any kids. So, y'all will either work it out or move on, but whatever happens will be for the best."

"Thanks, Arnold," she smiled.

"You know what I like to do late at night?" he asked, exhaling a plume of smoke and warm breath, "I like to look at the stars. Outer space blows my mind. Sometimes, I connect the dots to make pictures. I bet you could connect the dots to spell your name."

"Wow," she laughed, tilting her head toward the sky, "my name written in the stars! That seems appropriate for a goddess like me."

Judith traced constellations, attempting to create a J. The sky was clear and bright. She marveled at the moon, balancing atop naked trees on the mountain's summit. Everything from town all the way up to Rockhouse's mansion glowed in silver beams bouncing off snow. It was quite an enchanting sight. She noticed swings at the edge of the playground. All of them were red, except for one, blue oddball in the middle. Near the picnic shelter, at the playground's rear, a toppled trashcan spilled foam cups and cellophane packages. Through the picnic shelter, a man's shadow stretched long in moonlight. Snow fell from tree branches by the creek bank... Judith's eyes shot back to the shadow stretching through the shelter. Indeed, there was a man looming nearby. He wore a hooded sweatshirt, with the hood pulled snugly around his head. Although Judith could not make out his facial features, the man obviously peered in their direction, holding a slightly slumped stance, as if trying to hide from them. Once Judith's eyes made contact, she heard a strange, insect like clicking noise coming from his direction. Quickly, she turned away, her heart pounding with fear.

"Arnold," she whispered, "there's a man behind us."

"Where?" he asked, looking around.

"He's standing by the picnic shelter."

Arnold squinted and craned his neck.

"I don't see anybody."

Judith turned and he was gone, nowhere to be seen in the open field.

"That's impossible," she gasped, "He was right there. How did he get gone that fast?"

"Are you sure it wasn't just a shadow from a tree or something?"

"I looked right at him," she defended, "Let's get out of here. I'm starting to freak out."

Instantly, Arnold raised about two feet off the platform. He screamed and squirmed in terror. A gloved hand lifted Arnold in the air by the back of his neck, with brut force, unaltered by frantic flailing. The hooded man clicked like an excited insect, inches away from Judith's ear. She began to scream, but before sound could escape, the hooded man grasped her by the throat and pinned her to the ground. With his left hand, he held Arnold off the platform. His right hand anchored Judith in the mud. She could barely breathe, and her eyes felt like they were going to burst from their sockets. Judith kicked the man's armpit with every calorie of force she had. He did not even flinch against her attacks. The man's face rotated, until staring directly at Judith. Fright nearly paralyzed her heart. He *was* an insect. Beady red eyes flanked both sides of a wide, black snout. Tiny hairs tingled excitedly across leathery skin. A pincher-shaped fang extended from each side of his snout, clicking and vibrating with arousal. His drool slicked tongue lapped the air. She froze in shock. Arnold screamed enough for both of them. To Judith, it seemed she had been pinned there for hours. However, the entire scene unfolded in less than a minute. Still gazing at Judith, the creature casually brought Arnold's face to his snout. With a can opener like crunch, the beast's fangs clamped Arnold's throat. Blood squirted in every direction. Judith went into shock. She could not move or scream. The monster's jaws concaved as he sucked blood, pints at a time, from Arnold's jugular. His grip on Judith intensified with every gulp. Cold mud oozed into her ears. She struggled to fight the oncoming blackness, as her body began to shutdown. Arnold's screams receded into gurgles before death finally consumed him. Judith suddenly realized that this beast was a tick. He swelled with every swallow of blood, until his belly almost burst through the sweatshirt's zipper.

From the street, Shirley's piercing screams brought porch lights to life all through the trailer park. She cradled Brandon's head, hiding him from the horrific sight. Women in nightgowns and men in boxer shorts stormed from their trailers to answer Shirley's call of distress. The tick dropped Arnold's deflated body and released Judith. She gasped and coughed, fighting to regain full consciousness. The monster staggered drunkenly across the playground, his bloated body jiggling. Near the monkey bars, he collapsed to his knees, doubled over, and puked pints of Arnold's blood onto frosty grass. He no longer clicked like a bug. Instead, sobs of a human man thundered from his blood foundered guts. Judith sat straight up when she heard his cries. Perched on an elbow, with her swollen throat wheezing and strands of mud heavy hair clinging to tear streaked cheeks, Judith whispered, "No, it can't be."

A few feet away, Arnold lay lifeless. His eyeballs dangled on the bridge of his nose. There was little blood remaining to drip from his crushed jaw and mangled throat. Shirley continued screaming uncontrollably. One man exited his trailer with a shotgun, but before he could set his sights, the tick/man was gone in dead sprint across the playground. He jumped over the creek bank and disappeared.

A crowd swarmed Judith, bombarding her with questions, to which they received no reply. Blank faced and silent, she stared toward the creek bank, pondering the possibility of her suspicion that the bloodthirsty monster was Arthur.

4.

Amber wondered everyday what life was like before her great fall. She assumed "pre-fall" existence to be miserable, considering that she either ran far away from home, or no one at home cared enough to come looking for her. However, Amber occasionally fantasized of a past-life filled with passionate lovers and wild adventures. She struggled to grasp an identity. If the birth names of her body and spirit were revealed, which one would be appropriate to claim? Should memories surface in her mind, would they belong to her brain or her spirit? In the beginning, she approached RJ with these questions, and surprisingly, his answers offered comfort. But the truth was revealed, once Amber started sneaking necromancy books out of RJ's study. Zombies are monsters, not people. Very few zombies in recorded history had the ability to act even remotely human. Most were nothing more than moaning and limping carcasses. Experts never analyzed the dual identity of dead body and invoked spirit. For the most part, they simply deemed zombies mistakes of magical science that should be destroyed upon creation. Amber loved Mary Shelly's novel "Frankenstein" because it gave a character, to who she could relate. But even in Shelly's romantic tale, the articulate, love starved creation of Victor Frankenstein was considered a monster.

Deep emotional issues plagued Amber. Many factors contributed to her psychological distress. The struggle to form an identity of not only who she was, but also what she was, along with the knowledge of a short lifespan, vexed her daily. Amber panicked every time RJ sneezed, fearing that he had contracted a virus, which could kill him. Her nights were filled with worry that RJ might die in his sleep. An unstable personal life added extra injury to her wounded ego.

Boredom crippled her; hours upon hours alone with her thoughts. Teenage years were the worst. She longed for a social life. Yet Rockhouse, Benjamin, TV, and radio were her only companions. On TV, other teens indulged in carefree escapades. Their clothes and hairstyles were so cool. Eventually, admiration for girls on TV mutated into bitter jealousy. She retreated to existential melancholy and attempted to be as weird as possible. Doctoring and dressing dolls alleviated some of the depression. Amber lived vicariously through her creations. She fashioned them to mimic dates, sleepovers, and even sex.

RJ's wizardry skills were comparable to famous magicians, such as Merlin, Alistair Crowley, and Rasputin. In fact, had he chosen to document Amber's resurrection, it would arguably rank as the greatest act of necromancy since biblical times. RJ, however, possessed no ambition for fame. He occasionally consulted other wizards, but his greatest triumphs remained secret. Outside of a few tricky spells, he documented nothing. If a journal had been kept, it would have focused strictly on the science of necromancy, without devoting attention to the psychology of high functioning zombies. Wizards extend little concentration to the spiritual stability of their creations. In RJ's vast library, not one chapter existed to help Amber gain a better understanding of how to cope with emotional disorders of the living dead.

Then she met Kurt and felt happiness for the first time. But along with love, came frightening uncertainty. Kurt did not truly know Amber. She realized that he probably didn't believe her to actually be a zombie. More than likely, he figured she was a strange girl from a dysfunctional home, which was true. Kurt, however, had no idea how strange his new lover could be.

Amber often had conversations with herself for hours. She attempted suicide once by dunking her head in the toilet. Sometimes, temper tantrums resulted in fistfuls of hair yanked out of her head. When bouts of self-loathing reached climax, she wet the bed on purpose and slept in it. Amber understood that keeping a man like Kurt required curbing such dramatic outbursts. However, it would not be easy. For ten years, life presented no societal restraints for Amber. Suddenly, she needed to live within the boundaries of social acceptance. Yet she knew nothing of normal behavior, and there was no one to teach her.

Although Kurt was the first sexual partner she could remember, there had been other dates during her time with RJ. The internet provided a world wide web of lonely men desperate enough to settle for secret rendezvous on the breast of a creepy mountain. These men never seemed satisfactory to her. In many ways, they were weirder and more pathetic than she was. Most of her dates tried at least some level of physical romance. Amber wouldn't allow them past first base. Something about their desperation depressed her. The dates ended with awkward goodbyes and Amber walking the distance home. It never failed. Every internet suitor caused her to puke and consider suicide, once she had returned to the mansion.

Kurt came along and changed everything. He was her man. Even his imperfections seemed perfect. Had Kurt taken a crap on himself in public, Amber's perception of him would not have changed. She fell in love hard enough to vow, "No more suicide." Yet one question lingered. "Would love and a new life be enough to heal her bruised emotions?"

She considered leaving everything at the mansion and buying all new stuff, but if RJ cut her off financially, it would be unfair to lay the burden of funding a new wardrobe on Kurt. So, Amber boxed up her clothes and after much thought, decided to also take her dolls. She was too caught up in packing to realize when Big Daddy entered the room.

RJ slithered with the stealth of a shadow. Decades of silence and solitude withered him into a creeping-thing. He never knocked or announced his presence. Countless times, he entered the room during the most embarrassing moments for Amber. Locking the door did no good. Rockhouse possessed an uncanny knack for picking locks. He poured through every crack in the mansion like water. Even when he was miles away, Amber feared his impromptu entrance. The walls were eyes and ears, forbidding her the comfort of privacy.

On the evening she packed to leave, Amber left her bedroom door open. Although she dreaded it, a conversation with RJ was necessary. Life with him had been awkward and unfulfilling. Yet if someone said the word "father", RJ Rockhouse would be the only image to surface in Amber's mind.

In ten years, they never said "I love you". In fact, RJ never said much at all. His true feelings- if he had any- remained frozen in his heart. However, whether he liked it or not, should someone say the word "daughter", Amber's image would be the only one to surface in his mind.

For a couple of minutes, he stood silently, watching her stuff dolls into boxes. She stepped spryly across the room, almost dancing. Cheerfully smiling, her movements were song- a young woman lost in love- joy, excitement, uncertainty, and anticipation radiating from her eyes like a rainbow of emotion. The swan's sweet melody abruptly halted, when she pirouetted to find Old Codger lingering in the doorway like a spider.

"You scared me," she gasped.

"I hear you've been bribing the sheriff," he gurgled, slowly shuffling across hardwood, "have you earned any favors yet?"

"Don't talk like that, RJ. We just like each other; that's all."

Rockhouse crept closer. His cracked skin rippled with every step, white and thin like rice paper. High pitched wheezes rapidly pulsated. The odor of old man filled the room.

"Does he know about you?" he growled, limping toward her like a frail yet fierce troll, "I mean, does he know what you are?"

"Gee, you have such a sincere way of saying things," she scoffed, unaffected by his scare tactics, "He knows I'm different."

"Different? Is that what you call it?"

Rockhouse wore what he considered "a black cloak". To Amber, it looked more like a nightgown. Over and over, he tugged to keep it on his shoulders. For months at a time, he didn't change clothes. The cloak smelled so bad, not even washing it could eliminate the odor. RJ grew oblivious to his stench. Yet after a decade, Amber's nostrils still had not adapted to the putrid smell of decay.

"You're putting your things in boxes," he said, stretching his neck to see what all she had packed, "I guess you're leaving to be with him."

"Yes."

RJ stood level with her chin, his posture slumped like a C- quivering lips struggling to hold a snarl- cataract covered eyes a mixture of anger and exhaustion.

"You know what's going to happen, don't you?" he asked.

"Nobody ever really knows what's going to happen, RJ."

"Don't give me that! You know what I'm talking about, and you know exactly what is going to happen."

Amber bent to look him directly in the eyes and wagged her finger in front of his nose the way a mother would, while scolding a child.

"Yes I do. I'm leaving to be with Kurt, and whether it is for fifty years, one year, or five minutes, it will be the most happiness I've had in my entire life!"

The snarl left RJ's lips. His face drooped with sadness. Truthfully, as much as he attempted to convince Amber that he knew everything concerning her condition, he only knew one fact; she would die when he did. Other than that, she remained an enigma to him. The day he found her in the forest, RJ reacted on impulse. A simple spell was cast to try and save her. He hoped the spell would work but didn't expect it to... at least, not with such overwhelming success. At best, he figured she would gain a brief moment of consciousness to repent her sins. Most likely, he anticipated the spell would render a thoughtless robot, if it even worked at all. RJ never wished harm on Amber, but he certainly had not prepared for a simple, unsophisticated chant to produce a properly functioning teenaged daughter. Many old folks fear the younger generation. Rockhouse's creation definitely frightened him.

"I've done the best I can to make you happy, considering the situation," he argued.

Amber returned to her packing, refraining from looking at him or speaking with any emotion.

"I knew this conversation with you was coming. I'm not going to get angry or argue with you. This isn't about resentment, RJ. It's just about a guy."

RJ developed two tactics for dealing with Amber, whenever her behavior conflicted with his interests. Either he ignored her or tried to scare the hell of her. With suicide attempts, RJ chose to ignore the situation. He figured she wouldn't fail so many times, if her intensions were earnest. But when it came to love, Amber was serious as a heart attack, and Rockhouse knew it. So, as a final effort to scare some sense into her, RJ curled his fingers into claws and moved in front of Amber, growling and hissing, with his eyes twitching.

"It's been the same thing over and over since the day I moved you in here," he spat, "guys, guys, guys. That's all you've ever wanted."

For a brief second Amber froze, unblinking and leaning away from RJ the way one would standing near a coiled snake. Then, as if someone flipped a switch on, she burst into laughter.

"I'm a young woman! What do you expect? It's a wonder I never ran away. You wouldn't let me go to high school. You wouldn't let me get a job or go to college. I was forbidden to go on dates. Did you expect me to just sit in this room staring at the walls my whole life?"

Rockhouse showed his jagged, chipped teeth like a furious dog. Everywhere Amber went, he followed, continuing to groan and wheeze.

"You know what your problem is? You never listen to anything I say. That's your problem, Amber. If you had gone to high school, you would have been the most picked on kid there. You're RJ Rockhouse's adopted child. That alone would have had you branded a freak right from the start. Then add on your personality disorders and the other kids' jealousy of your money and high school would have been a living hell for you. There's no way you could have finished college or held onto a job with your personality problems and you know it."

She spun on her heels, mocking RJ's growl, with a finger jabbing his bony ribs.

"Since we're talking about my problems, why don't we talk about yours, too? You know what your problem is? YOU'RE COMPLETELY INSANE! That's your problem, RJ. Can't you see it? Don't you realize that things in this house aren't right? Seriously, how many murders have you committed?"

He smacked her finger away and arrogantly turned up his nose.

"A few people have lost their lives by my bidding, but that was decades before you were born."

"Oh, well I guess I'm wrong," she yelled, waving her hands, "You're not crazy. You've only murdered a few people. How many cadavers have you toyed with down in the basement? There have probably been too many to count. Normal families do not have cadavers delivered to their houses. Normal families do not try to bring the dead back to life. They don't cast spells on coyotes or drink blood. I have seen all of these things in this house!"

RJ's nose lowered. He stared at her with annoyed disgust. Arguing with Amber proved to be a difficult task. For, as sure as RJ spoke truth, Amber's words were also honest. As a zombie, she could never live the life of a normal person. Yet she was a normal person. Amber had a heart, soul, and everything that comes along with these traits. Outside of a few personality disorders, she appeared to be nothing more than a beautiful, young woman. But nature has a formula, and when the recipe is altered, things go awry. Confusion and chaos surrounded her existence. No logic could be developed; no structure formed.

Every situation involving Amber became a paradox, where each answer created a million more questions, like an argument, in which both participants are equally right or wrong.

"You were never hurt or even placed in harm's way," RJ responded.

"Hey, I don't doubt that you care for me and want to keep me safe," she groaned, clutching her forehead, "All of the friction we've ever had comes from this. I am a young woman. You are an old man, and you refuse to accept that I do not want the same things you want for me. I don't care about money. I don't want to be a witch. And I don't want to live forever. All I want is to be normal."

"Well, that's too bad, Amber, because normal is something you cannot be. There were only two options for you. You could either die back there on the mountain or die when I do. Normal people die once, not twice, Amber. If your life was normal right now, you'd be dead."

She spat on the floor and flipped him off. Amber often burst into tantrums when RJ interfered with her desires. The fits occurred more frequently during her teenage years. However, Amber never had a circumstance like the one she created with Kurt. She would cuss, scream insults, and shatter windows to get her way. He measured her emotional distress with great caution.

"All I want to say to you is this," she barked, "if I only have one day of life left, please let me live it."

"Letting you go isn't the hard part," he chuckled, "The hard part is knowing how it will turn out. If I let you loose into the world, you will hurt and confuse everyone you make contact with and eventually come crawling back home with your tail tucked between your legs, leaving a big mess that I will have to clean up."

She spat in his face, right between the eyes. RJ's little girl grew up to be a devil in angel's skin; a rabid wolf in a poodle's wrapping. There she stood, her face scarlet with anger, breathing like a woman in labor. The poor, little, rich girl had the "eccentric" thing perfected. Her gray sweatshirt was cut to showcase her midriff. One sleeve stretched to her wrist. The other had been completely sliced off. A white, sequined belt wrapped around her waist, holding up a pair of baggy, maroon sweatpants. She looked like a sexy freak, and that is exactly what she was. Amber might have been pretty, but inside that cute head, a zombie's psyche festered.

"Oh, trust me," she huffed, "when I leave, I'm gone."

"No you're not," he scorned, ignoring the spit dangling between his eyes, "and you know why? You are like a dog on a chain in the yard. The chain keeps you from doing anything. I feed you. I give you shelter and keep you safe. Without me, you are nothing, like a dog on a chain."

Amber backed away from him with fire in her eyes. She reached under her shirt and removed her bra. Then, she walked over to a lit candle on the end table, sat the bra ablaze, and threw it at RJ's face.

"Well, this old bitch is breaking her chain today!" she howled.

RJ stomped out the fire and shook his head.

"After ten years, you should understand this better than anybody. Your chain cannot be broken. Wherever you go, the chain will go with you."

"Then I guess that's something I'm just going to have to deal with. I'm a grown woman, RJ. I don't need you to protect me from the world anymore."

"You don't get it, do you? It's not you I'm trying to protect."

"Then who is it?"

"It's them," he shouted so violently, he almost collapsed, "the boyfriends... the sheriff. Do you know what you are about to do to that man? You are giving false hope. He will feel the heat of your body and hear the sweetness of your voice. He will share his heart with you and maybe start planning a life that revolves around you. Then do you know what's going to happen? You are going to die, and he will become a shell of a man! That's what happened to me. Why do you think my life has been so miserable and things in this house aren't right? It is because, when I was a young man, I dared to share my heart with a woman, and she shared her heart with me. No sooner than the bond was created, she died and left me alone forever."

Amber's face remained red, but not with wrath. Her lips curved into frown. Tears swelled in her eyes. She sat on the bed, subdued with sadness. RJ reseeded to her level of emotion.

"But you are a grown woman," he sighed, "If you want to leave, I won't try to stop you or give you any problems. You can take all of your things or leave them here. I don't care. Call the sheriff right now, if you want."

He limped toward the door, mumbling something, most likely a protection spell. The hem of his black cloak slithered across the floor. Amber pulled her knees up to her chest and rocked back and forth, weeping profusely.

"I don't know what to do," she sobbed, "I love him, daddy."

RJ turned to look at her. His eyes were too old to cry and his voice too worn to sooth. Even so, an aura of sincerity surrounded him. Deep inside, he understood that all of Amber's misery was his fault.

"I know you do," he answered softly, "All you ever wanted was to find love. Now that you've found it, there is a hard question for you to answer. Do you break his heart or your own?"

He walked away. Amber wondered if she would ever see him again. She couldn't help but feel guilty. It was only two days until RJ's 100th birthday. A couple more midnights brought a milestone for him that few achieve; a century of life on planet Earth. But he never made a big deal out of birthdays, his or anyone else's. There were no plans for ice cream and cake. So, she wondered why he even argued to keep her there. With all the headache she'd caused him throughout the years, it seemed he would want her gone.

Amber cried on the bed for a long while, soaking in images of her domain. As much as she wanted to leave, part of her would miss that bedroom. For ten years, it served as her kingdom. The room was large, with high walls, each one painted a different color. The floor spread wide enough to host a ball. But a large room makes for a small world. There was a lot to do and little time in which to do it. Amber knew she had to say goodbye.

She took a walk through the backyard to clear her head. The air was still cold but noticeably warmer than it had been the day before. For the first time in over a week, patches of green were visible on the lawn. Her snowman looked pitiful. One twig-arm had fallen to the ground. The smoking pipe and button eyes were gone. Frosty's slushy head lost its form. Basically, he became a mound of melting snow, with RJ's top hat desperately clinging to the summit. The sight of her deformed snowman once again brought tears to Amber's eyes. Back and forth she teetered from excitement to dread. Something powerful waited on the near horizon. She wondered if the changing weather foretold of new life or certain death.

5.

Arthur parked in front of Rockhouse Manor, feeling oddly peaceful for a man about to enter the spookiest house in perhaps all of Appalachia. Crisp morning air frosted patches of the mountains, which were not still covered with snow. It had been a long time since Arthur looked so dapper. A charcoal colored trench coat draped from his shoulders. Underneath the coat, a silver button up shirt was tucked tightly into smooth, black slacks. His loafers clicked along the cobblestone walkway. Clean shaven, with eyes behind black shades, he chewed gum to the rhythm of his stride. Arthur stared out over the yard. He was the first outsider ever to notice that trees within the walkway's circumference were aligned to form an imaginary pentagram.

Ice incased the front steps, but Arthur skipped up them with no problems. The door didn't have a buzzer. So, he clanged the cathead knocker at least a dozen times and waited about five minutes before someone finally answered the door.

Benjamin stood in the doorway, wearing the same outfit he had on when Arthur last saw him. There was no "hello" or "may I help you" to acknowledge the visitor's presence. Benjamin probably would have stood still and silent until one of them collapsed had Arthur not spoke.

"Hi," he chirped, "I'm Arthur Addler from down in the trailer park. Mr. Rockhouse asked me to get in touch with him"

Benjamin peered straight ahead, his face a rugged wax mold, with stone shoulders and chest showing no signs of breathing.

"May I come in?"

"There's no need," a frail, coarse voice called from within the mansion.

Benjamin slid to the side, and the mouse-like frame of RJ Rockhouse limped into the doorway's light. The smells of aging-mildew, dust, and slight decay- followed Rockhouse across the room. His icicle smile stretched wide and quivering hands came together in feeble attempt to clap approvingly.

"You do not need to come in," he gurgled, "all you need to do is simply say yes or no."

"When is your birthday?" Arthur asked.

"Tomorrow," Rockhouse excitedly answered, "you will need to be here at eight o'clock in the morning."

"Okay," Arthur confirmed, "I've thought about it, and my answer is yes."

Rockhouse raised a trembling hand high, as if sending praise to Heaven. A frosty, crystal tear dangled at the edge of his doughy, wrinkled eyelid.

"Something told me you would come today.Congratulations, Arthur Addler, you just won the lottery."

"I wanted to give this as much thought as possible," Arthur explained.

Rockhouse shuffled closer. Arthur feared those flabby, old man lips were about to kiss him. Instead, he softly poked Arthur between the breasts. Rockhouse's fingers felt like toothpicks. His breath became mist in the cold winter air, rising to brush Arthur's face like ghostly hands.

"How is Judith?" RJ queried.

"She's okay, I guess."

"The poor thing must be traumatized."

"Why do you say that?"

"For God's sake," he gasped, his wrinkles rising with shock, "she watched a man get mutilated and was nearly murdered herself."

"Oh yeah," Arthur nervously squeaked, "the murder. That was horrible."

Rockhouse's beady eyes shaped to form a puzzling expression, roaming up and down from Arthur's head to his toes. He appeared to be sizing Arthur up. Apparently, whatever he was looking for escaped radar because the puzzlement melted from RJ's face and gentle concern returned.

"Is she staying at home, or did she leave the trailer park?"

"To tell you the truth, sir, I haven't talked to her since the murder. We had a bad fight a few days ago. I went to stay with my brother. But Judith really doesn't have anywhere else to go. So, to the best of my knowledge, she's still there."

"Good," he purred, with a slobbery grin, "she is safer there."

The same baffled expression chiseled into RJ's wrinkles a few seconds earlier now consumed Arthur. However, he didn't need to size RJ up. Every warning imaginable flashed on Arthur's radar, whenever Rockhouse entered the scene.

"Why do you say she's safer in the trailer park?"

"The beast might be ugly and bloodthirsty," Rockhouse excitedly whispered, "but it is also smart and cautious. The police are guarding Sugarland tightly. When the beast strikes again, it will not be there."

"Beast?" Arthur inquired.

"Mr. Addler, you might think I'm a crazy, old man. And you know what, you might be correct in that assumption. But heed my wisdom. We have a vampire on the loose in this town."

To RJ's surprise, Arthur did not speak. Instead, he softly nodded in agreement.

"Vampires don't like to draw attention," Rockhouse continued, "So it might not attack here again. But to be on the safe side, you should fashion a pointed, wooden cross and carry it around with you at all times. Should you encounter the beast, stab it with the cross, right through its heart."

Yellow, cracked fingernails jabbed the center of Arthur's breast. Rockhouse winked and smiled.

"But Judith is safest at home," said RJ, "the beast didn't strike because he has his sights set on her. He was simply hungry. It could've been anyone. Let me give you some advice, too, Arthur. You've gone this long without talking to her. Give the silence one more night. Tomorrow morning, after I am gone, you will become one of the wealthiest men in all of this state. That kind of money helps ease a woman's fury."

Arthur removed his shades and stuffed them in the trench coat's pocket. With a gravely serious gaze, he peered down into RJ's misty eyes.

"Tell me how you want this done," Arthur requested.

Rockhouse laughed. He had to raise his arm in order to put a hand on Arthur's shoulder. The cold breeze blew up RJ's cloak, sending the smell of death straight into Arthur's sinuses.

"I really don't care," Rockhouse coughed, "just make it as unsuspicious as possible."

Arthur left, with the odor of death clinging to his trench coat. Like the spray of a skunk, the scent followed him all day. Deep seriousness embedded in both men's eyes throughout the conversation. Chill bumps tiled their bodies, and it wasn't because of the wind. They well perceived the situation's intensity. The clock ticked hastily, as if its hands were overly greased. One question owned each lightening fast hour. "Would Arthur have the will power to do it?"

Fourth Quarter
Misery is a Vampire
1.

Sheriff Bochester stood before the window in his office, soaking up sunlight. He needed energy. Twelve hours earlier he examined a body so mangled, it could have been a deer or small bear. However, it was no animal. The corpse belonged to a young boy from a few miles down the road. Kurt could not shake off the vision of Arnold's head dangling at the end of his spine, with his throat completely hollowed out- meat, skin, veins, and everything, devoured like candy- eyeballs twisted up in optic nerves, severed from their sockets on the muddy ground. Had there been no witnesses, Kurt would have sworn the perpetrator to be a wild beast or even a monster. There was no way imaginable for a person to accomplish such a deed. But there were several witnesses to the crime, one of whom saw the entire act from merely inches away. The testimony of Judith Page sat at the center of his desk. According to her, the murderer wore the mask of a monster, but was human without any doubt. Who could possess such strength?

Arnold's murder became infamously known as the most horrific in local history, and the man responsible remained on the loose, more than likely right there in town. If he completely mutilated a grown man in merely seconds, Kurt figured he would probably swallow a small child with one bite.

The sheriff could not afford to get frustrated. Too many people needed his protection more than ever. But it seemed to Kurt that the weight on his shoulders might break him. With each day, the blizzard's aftermath receded further, yet no word from EJ. He had the responsibility of solving the worst crime in county history. Last but not least, Amber awaited rescue.

Kurt walked out of his office, to the front desk, where Deputy Collins shuffled through paperwork. Collins was Sheriff Bochester's right hand man. His intelligent, laid back demeanor appealed to Kurt. He provided welcomed advice on almost every matter, should the situation involve law enforcement or politics.

"Collins, are you familiar with RJ Rockhouse?"

The deputy removed his glasses, reared back in the chair, and firmly massaged his bare scalp.

"I know who he his," Collins groaned, stretching his back, "but I've never met him"

"Have you ever heard any stories about him?"

"My cousin used to work at the mental ward RJ's brother is locked up in. He tells some crazy stories about working there."

Kurt pulled up a chair and leaned across the desk secretively, as he sat.

"RJ has a brother?"

"Yes. His name is Randy Rockhouse. My cousin has never been known to spread tall tales, but he swears to be damned that Randy Rockhouse is a vampire."

"Really?"

"Oh yeah," Collins chuckled, "it's a hard story to swallow. They have to feed Randy blood to keep him alive. He still looks like a man in his forties, even though he's probably about ninety. But this is the part of the story I never could believe. He said that as long as they fed Randy animal blood, everything was fine, but if he smelled human blood, he would start changing into a man-sized mosquito."

Collins expected the sheriff to laugh. Instead, his face turned lily white and his jaw dropped wide open.

"I'll be damned," Kurt gasped.

"My cousin swears he saw it happen. He'd turn into a mosquito and stay that way for a little while. It's the weirdest story I've ever heard."

"RJ has an adopted daughter," Kurt informed, "Have you heard anything about her?"

"I've heard she's good looking and a little strange acting," Collins replied, "Are you thinking they might be involved in that murder last night?"

"There's no way an old man or a woman could have done that," Kurt scoffed, "I just wonder about the whole situation up there at the trailer park. What's the name of that mental hospital?"

"I think it's called Hillside Behavioral Institute. It's just across the border from Louisville."

Kurt found the address, called to inform Amber it would be evening before he could pick her up, and then was on his way to Hillside Behavioral Institute to question what he believed would be a real life vampire.

Hillside resembled the typical nut house. There were flowerbeds and bushes in the yard. In spring and summer, the place probably looked cheery. However, winter's harshness killed all of nature's colors, except brown. The two story structure, made of gray block, branched off into wings at each side, with windows evenly lined every twelve feet across the diameter. A red, pointed roof unsuccessfully attempted to give the psychiatric center a homey presence.

The inside looked less like a home and more like a hospital. Teal blocks lined the halls, along with white tile on the floor. Fluorescent bulbs ran across the ceiling of each corridor. The halls smelled of cheap, lemony cleaning solution.

Kurt's badge granted easy access into the institute director's office. His nameplate read, "Dr. Jenkins". Right away, Kurt deduced that Doctor Jenkins was the kind of man who still lived at home with mama, despite an impressive degree and high level position in psychiatrics. Jenkins was a short, pudgy fellow, with thick glasses, thin moustache, and a chrome dome. Clippings from Spider-Man, Superman, and Incredible Hulk comic books were framed on his office walls like certificates of excellence.

"Welcome... Sheriff Bochester is it?" he nervously stammered, shaking Kurt's hand, as he entered the office.

"Yes, doctor," Kurt answered, removing his derby and giving Jenkins' hand a firm squeeze, "interesting office. I wish I could have fun with the sheriff's office like you have here."

"In a place like this, you've got to have a little fun to keep yourself sane," Jenkins cackled annoyingly, "Do you like comic books?"

"I watch all the movies. I never collected comic books, though."

Doctor Jenkins' face lit up, and he actually gasped.

"You've got to see what I've got here," he exclaimed, motioning for the sheriff to follow. Kurt cast a dumbfounded look and amusedly trailed the doctor.

Jenkins led him to a large entertainment center against the left wall. The contents were rather over indulgent for the office of a nine to five man... plasma TV, X-Box 360, laptop complete with Netflix, superhero action figures, and an aquarium full of exotic fish. Kurt guessed that Jenkins spent a lot of time in his office, even when he was off the clock.

"These are rare," Jenkins boasted, opening a drawer full of comic books bound in plastic sleeves, "These are my least prized ones. That's why they're here in the office instead of my vault at home, but they're still pretty impressive."

"You are a blessed man," Kurt smiled.

"I've got movies you've probably never even heard of. Some of my movies are no longer in print. I've got foreign bootlegs and rare director's cuts. Hey, if you like zombie movies, I can hook you up with a killer website that can get you anything you need."

Jenkins spoke of sci-fi paraphernalia the way dope dealers talked about primo cocaine.

"Zombie movies," Kurt laughed, for reasons Jenkins never could have imagined, "let me tell you, I love zombies. But I don't get much time for movies. This is a cool collection, though."

Jenkins beamed with pride.

"Thanks, but I'm sure you didn't drive here to talk with me about zombies. How can we be of service to you, sheriff?"

He crossed the room to his desk and took a seat. Kurt followed.

"I'm investigating a gruesome murder, doctor. It happened last night in my hometown. I think one of your patients might have some information that can help me."

Jenkins seemed exited by thoughts of participating in a murder investigation.

"Really?" he squeaked, "Which patient?"

"Randy Rockhouse."

The doctor's jaw dropped and his face turned purple. He opened the desk drawer and fumbled around until finding a grape Blow-Pop. Within the snap of a finger, the sucker was unwrapped and thrusting back and forth through his mouth like a toothbrush.

"Randy Rochouse," he gagged, "he can't help you."

"Why not?"

"He is in maximum security. He has very little contact with the outside world. It would be impossible for Randy Rockhouse to have any information pertaining to your case."

Kurt put his fists on Jenkins' desk and flexed his biceps.

"I'd like to question him anyway."

"Sorry, sheriff, I cannot allow you to see him."

"Doctor, if I have to leave here without talking to Randy Rockhouse, you can bet your X-Men panties, I'll be pissed off. I will get a warrant, and I will call the media."

"Can you get a warrant against the FBI?" Jenkins snorted, like a hopeless nerd, "Because Randy Rockhouse is government property. We simply house him. If you want clearance, call the president."

Kurt relaxed. He scanned the room, not paying attention to anything. Two truths became obvious to him. He was in over his head, and he was bound by the badge and his heart to delve in deeper than he should go. He pulled a checkbook from inside his coat pocket.

"How much?" Kurt asked.

"What are you talking about?"

"How much for one hour with Rockhouse?"

"Sheriff, bribes are illegal."

"So are bootlegged movies," Kurt growled, "I might not be FBI, but you can damn well bet I've got connections. If I leave here without talking to Randy Rockhouse, you will get searched for copyright infringement. Boy, I ain't playing. Now, I'm gonna write you a check with no strings attached, or I can leave here pissed. It's your call, doc."

Jenkins took a long, hard gulp. Kurt would have bet that the doctor trickled in his briefs. He sat for a moment, nervously taping fingernails on the desk.

"You'll have to sign a waiver," Jenkins whimpered, almost in tears.

Doctor Higgins led Kurt downstairs. Higgins, unlike Jenkins, was the epitome of cool. He walked with a confident, laid back strut. An African-American, in his mid-thirties, he had the Tom Selleck moustache with high and tight hairdo. Higgins seemed neither intimidated nor disrespectful toward the sheriff. Their walk descended about a million steps, into a dungeon-like lair, void of natural light. Along the way, conversation was candid, exactly the way Sheriff Bochester liked it.

"That Jenkins guy," Kurt groaned, "what's the deal with him?"

"Jenkins is good at his job," Higgins defended, "He's a little strange, but good psychologists usually are. Off the record, I think he might be a closet homo."

Kurt laughed out loud. The sound echoed down a dim, teal corridor that appeared to stretch for miles.

"But seriously, sheriff, you need to be prepared for what you are about to step into. Randy Rockhouse ain't no run of the mill nut job. He's a vampire, my man. Now, you might not believe in vampires, but you better get yourself as close to believing in them as you can before you enter a room with him. He'll eat your face and brag about it."

"Let me ask you something, and be straight with me," Kurt demanded, "Does he really mutate when he smells human blood?"

"Yes," Doctor Higgins answered in a way that made Kurt believe him, "but the government handles all that business now. We never give him human blood. The feds come in here every so often and do tests on him. All that jazz is top secret and off limits to us. I tell you, I don't know what scares me worse, Randy's existence or the fact that our government is studying it."

They walked on through the basement's bowels, following sewer pipes and mildewed floor tiles. The lights dimmed more and more with each step. There were no doors or branching hallways. The scene reminded Kurt of a bunker.

"Am I gonna die in here?" Kurt asked.

"We're taking precautions to make sure that doesn't happen. But, honestly, sheriff, I can't answer that question. He has no conscience. I don't know what his intensions will be. But everything he does is evil. Just watch yourself, man, and don't spend more time with him than you need to."

"Will he be shackled?"

"Yes, but you've gotta watch him. He's crafty. You should also know that he's been given a dog to keep him calm."

"A dog?"

"Yes, and he'll probably eat it right in front of you. If you get too freaked out, just holler. We'll be watching through the double sided mirror."

"Hey, Higgins, is he a vampire for real?"

Higgins stopped walking. Without the click of their heels, the atmosphere turned deadly silent.

"Listen, sheriff," Doctor Higgins said coldly, wide eyes never blinking, "I didn't believe in vampires until I met Randy Rockhouse. This is for real. The worst thing you can do right now is enter that room a skeptic."

They continued down the hallway. Kurt was in good shape, but they walked far enough for him to get winded. Finally, a silver, metal door appeared at the left of the hall; no window or I.D. plate.

"Sheriff, why do you want to talk to this monster?" Higgins asked, grasping Kurt by the arm.

"There was a murder in my town last night. Witnesses say a man committed the crime, but the victim's throat was completely devoured. All and all, the murder took about a minute."

Doctor Higgins nodded.

"If I didn't know Randy was secured here all night, I'd swear he did it. I hope you find what you're looking for. God be with you, sheriff."

Higgins opened the door. Randy sat on a cot in the corner. A harness was rigged around his torso, connected to a six foot chain, which extended from a thick steal ring on the wall. He wore standard, lime green scrubs with cloth slippers, the same color. Jet black hair streamed down his shoulders. Sure enough, he looked like a handsome man in his forties- dark eyes, pale skin, and rugged jaw.

"Please come in, Sheriff Bochester," he welcomed, with a deep, soothing voice.

Kurt stepped inside, and the door immediately clanged shut behind him. A tiny poodle scampered happily up to Kurt's boots, wagging its tail.

"They've set up a table for you to use incase you need to take notes or anything," Randy said, "Please, have a seat."

Kurt sat at the small table on the opposite side of the room. The poodle followed. He gave it a couple of loving pats on the head.

"I apologize for the dog," Randy continued, "situations like this are the only time I get to call some of the shots. They want me to be happy so I don't kill you. When these instances come around, I like to make as many outlandish requests as possible."

Kurt heeded Doctor Higgins' advice and cut right to the chase.

"RJ Rockhouse is your brother, correct?"

"That's right. He will turn the big 1-0-0 tomorrow. You really couldn't have shown up at a more perfect time."

"Is he a vampire, too?"

"No, he's a warlock; a necromancer to be more specific."

"Did he turn you into a vampire?"

"Yes, but I asked him to. I found a vampire creation spell. But one cannot cast the spell on one's self. So, I made RJ do it for me."

The vampire probably smelled Kurt's fear. A sleazy grin stretched across Randy's face. Tiny, white nubs slightly protruded above his eyeteeth. Kurt assumed that blood was heavy on Randy's mind, and the faintest hint of it would seduce those tiny nubs into sprouting fangs.

"Do you know why I'm here?" Kurt asked.

"Not exactly."

"There was a murder last night in the trailer park right below RJ's mansion. He owns the trailer park, in fact. I believe this murder was committed by a vampire."

"Were there bite marks on the neck?"

"There was no neck. It got devoured in about a minute."

Randy stood and paced in front of the bed, strolling in each direction until the harness stopped him. Apparently, when vampires are excited, fangs aren't the only things aroused. His scrub pants revealed a happy lump from within. When Randy noticed the "wooden stake" rising to salute, he blushed, quickly leapt onto the cot, and crossed his legs.

"It was a vampire," he squeaked, "I'm going to guess your bloodsucker is a tick. It could have been a bat, but bats are a little more sophisticated. So, I'm guessing it was a tick."

"What do you mean?"

Randy slowly scratched his throat, smiling and staring at Kurt. His skin was white and smooth as paper. Coal black hair tumbled in thick waves across firm shoulders. On the outside, ladies would have loved him, until they discovered him to be an almost ninety-year old mosquito mutant.

"Vampirism is different from the way Hollywood portrays it," he proudly instructed, "Some things are the same, but most is just fabrication. It's actually a wooden cross through the heart or beheading that kills vampires. Any other effort to kill us will fail... well, except for starvation. However, we are not immortal. Vampires have long life spans, sometimes over a thousand years. But we are still human in essence. So, we will eventually die of natural causes if nothing else kills us. Sunlight and garlic doesn't bother us. Neither does holy water. Actually, some vampires get baptized and try to live a life for God. It's a difficult lifestyle.

Some consider vampirism a blessing. Most believe it to be a curse. Basically, we get hungry for the same kind of food you do-meat, vegetables, bread. But we also must have a regular diet of blood to stay alive. It can be any kind of blood. If the blood is animal or insect, we drink it the same way you would wine. If the blood is human, we mutate into a parasite."

"Why does human blood turn you that way?"

"It's just part of the curse. There are two types of vampire, pure-breed and parasite. Your throat eating perpetrator and I belong to the parasite family. Some of us are leeches, ticks, mosquitoes, bats... the list goes on. Most vamps are pure-breeds. They just turn into nasty looking freaks, with fangs, claws, and reptilian tongues. When human blood is involved, there are no sexy vampires. It's the scariest thing you'll ever see."

"What determines which ones will be pure-breed and which will be parasite?"

"Pure-breeds carry vampirism like a virus. They suck blood by biting their victims on the neck or wrist... whatever. Most times, their victims die, but every now and then, a victim will stay alive just long enough for the virus to incubate. When that happens, the victim has become a pure-breed vampire. Parasites have never been bitten. A sorcerer or sorceress casts a spell to turn a person into a parasite."

The poodle trotted happily about the room, wagging its bobtail. A yellow line crossed the floor, approximately nine feet from Randy's cot, marking the "unsafe" area. Kurt thought to himself, "They forgot to tell me about the line." Apparently, they also failed to inform the dog. It pranced into unfriendly territory. Randy scooped the poodle in one hand and cradled it lovingly against his chest, softly stroking thick, white fur. The dog licked his hand, oblivious to awaiting danger.

"There's one problem I'm having, Randy. In my time as a law enforcement officer, there have been a handful of murders in town, but they were all from gunshots, stabbings, and typical stuff like that. This is the only case that could have been done by a vampire. When it comes to supernatural crimes in our little town, all fingers point to your brother."

"I think I'll name her puddin'," Randy said of the dog, "She's just so sweet."

He laughed and charmed Puddin' with baby talk for a few seconds before acknowledging Kurt's comment.

"Sheriff, if you think RJ is involved in this crime, he is the one you should question, not me."

Randy held Puddin' close. The dog bathed his face with affectionate licks. All the while, the vampire laughed.

"There is something I know," Randy giggled, "you're not just here to ask about a murder. There is an ulterior motive for your visit with me today. I want you to tell me what that motive is, but be careful what you say. Big Brother is watching."

Randy pointed to the reversible mirror.

"What makes you think I have ulterior motives?" Kurt asked.

"I just know," Randy sighed, "and here's the deal. If you tell me the truth about why you're here, I'll let this dog go. If you lie to me, I'll eat it alive. How compassionate are you, sheriff?"

"How will you know if I'm lying?"

"I'll know by applying many of the same techniques you cops use."

Puddin' almost fell asleep in the comforting safety of Randy's embrace. The vampire had no remorse manipulating a dog. Kurt realized that he would probably have less remorse tricking him. But there was nowhere else to turn. Kurt figured as long as he made it out of there with his face attached, the day wouldn't be a total loss.

"RJ's daughter is moving in with me tonight."

Randy smiled wickedly and released the dog.

"How wonderful," he purred.

"Why do you say that?"

Randy scooted forward to the edge of the cot, wringing his hands and bowing so that hair draped over his face. His voice became a steady buzz.

"Since RJ's wife died, seventy-five years ago, he has been anxiously preparing for tomorrow. He turns one hundred, and this is a very significant day for him."

"I'm assuming he has some kind of witchcraft in the works," Kurt coaxed.

"Yes," Randy's buzz excitedly accelerated, "in accordance with the laws of sorcery, a necromancer can only resurrect his own spirit on his 100th birthday."

"Meaning what?"

"His plan is to bring his wife's spirit back into a body. He will also resurrect his spirit so that they can once again be together."

"Okay," Kurt interjected, "so, basically, he's going to dig up a couple of corpses. That's a creepy crime, but not the worst of crimes."

Randy angrily stood, flipping hair away from his face, snarling and drooling, with breaths pounding in his chest.

"You don't understand," he growled, "this is a well calculated plan! He isn't going to dig up half rotted corpses. The bodies will be fresh, as in freshly murdered."

Kurt removed his derby and leaned back in the chair, crossing his arms, and trying hard not to show fear or excitement.

"You have my attention," he conceded.

Randy began to slightly shake, as he once again paced. His eyes rotated all about like there were a million thoughts flashing in his head and he was attempting to glimpse all of them. The mosquito buzz now thundered from his throat.

"The trailer park is just a cattle call," he stated, with sweat beginning to pour down his face, "he brought in poor people- low lives. From them, he intends to pick his victims. There is no doubt he has already selected a couple and drawn up a will, leaving them his fortune."

"I see," Kurt laughed, "he's willing them his money so that he will still have it after all this resurrection business."

Randy stopped pacing and gave Kurt a desperate, almost sad look.

"That's right. You need some advice, sheriff, and I'm the best person to give it to you."

"I'm all ears," Kurt invited.

"If you want my advice," he whimpered painfully, "you'll have to give me back the dog."

Randy's hungry eyes and inhuman hum indicated to Kurt that playtime had ended. He stood, put on his derby, and headed for the door.

"Thanks for your help," he said, "I don't really need any advice. There's a murder to stop and I have little time to do it."

"It's about Amber," Randy teased, "and it is something you really should know."

Kurt turned to stare at Randy, shaking and slouching

pathetically at the foot of his cot. Then he took a moment to peer into the mirror along the rear wall. Puddin' hopped around Kurt's boots. He picked up the happy dog and held it out toward Randy, whose bloodshot eyes lit up, as his posture popped erect. As Randy frantically lunged, the harness yanked breath from his chest, leaving his outstretched fingers only inches away from satisfaction.

"Advice first," Kurt ordered, "then you get the dog."

Randy retreated back to the foot of his cot, mouthing profanities. His expression showed pure hatred and misery. Stubbly hairs popped from the pours on his face, and his eyes turned yellow.

"She's going to die when RJ dies," he growled, tongue lapping the air, "He resurrected her from the dead, so their spirits are bound within necromancy. When he dies, she will, too. But if he resurrects his own spirit, it will be a transformation from one host to another. In other words, he isn't going to die on his birthday. His spirit will simply change bodies. So, what do you do, sheriff? If you stop RJ, he won't live another year, meaning your lover won't live another year. If you don't stop RJ, he will have life renewed, so will Amber. But this redemption can only come from you turning your back on the cold blooded murder of an innocent, young couple. It's an interesting dilemma for a sheriff. Whose life do you save?"

The glare of Kurt's eyes could have cut stone. He peered at Randy with a mean countenance that said, "I don't care if you are a vampire. I'll rip your freakin' head off." Randy stood still, with a ghostly, half scared expression.

"I'm ready to leave," Kurt shouted at the mirror.

"The dog," Randy squealed, "you promised. You're a liar! You're a pig and a liar. I hope Amber dies in your arms, you low life crook!"

Kurt bit the top knuckle of his middle finger, just hard enough to make it bleed. Using the same finger, he flipped Randy off, with a tear-sized bead of blood trickling toward his hand. The vampire shrieked and hit the floor; his legs kicking wildly, fingers stiffly curled, gnawing on his tongue like a man in the middle of a violent seizure. The back of Randy's scrub top tore open, freeing a large, bow-shaped wing, webbed with pulsating veins. Uncontrollably, his wing batted the floor. Randy flipped onto his knees, bloody gums peeling open to reveal saw tooth fangs. A hose-like tongue shot from his jaws and extended all the way to Kurt's face, flapping around his eyes in attempt to suck them from their sockets. Slime splattered across Kurt's forehead into his hair.

The door opened and a team of aides quickly rushed Kurt (still holding Puddin') into the hall. They panicked and cursed, slamming the steel door shut and frantically jolting in every direction to make sure all possible exits from the building were firmly secured. The sound of Randy's metamorphosis was loud enough to echo down the hall, even from behind a steel door. Bones and joints popped like shotgun fire as they transformed. Bubbling gelatin sounds gurgled and wheezed on the other side of the steel. Randy's screams melted into a high pitched insect buzz.

Kurt was aware of the scene unfolding around him, but paid the terrifying chaos no mind. Puddin' wiggled from his grasp and disappeared with a horrified sprint down the hall. Kurt leaned against the wall, holding his stomach. As hard as he tried, he could not fight off vomit. On the brink of a tear filled nervous breakdown, he puked all over the floor. Doctors and aides thought he was overcome with fear, and they were right, but not for the reasons they assumed.

When he first became sheriff, Kurt held aspirations of handling the county's most difficult decisions. Now that those ambitions had reached fruition, would he be a law enforcer and protect the innocent or would he be a politician and protect his own interests? Kurt had only a matter of hours to decide.

2.

When Arthur's brother, Jerry, called Judith's cell phone and asked if she would meet him at her trailer, she didn't really know how to feel. She had suspicions that Arthur might have been the monster, which murdered Arnold and nearly killed her, but perhaps it was somebody- or something- else. Arnold had been dead less than a day. Already she spoke to the police and a host of family. It was apparent to everyone, including Judith, that witnessing the incident drove her borderline insane. Every time the wind blew or an appliance kicked on, she almost jumped out of her skin. She couldn't eat or sleep. All Judith could do was pace back and forth across the floor, crying and smoking one cigarette after another.

She loved Arthur and didn't want to falsely accuse him, but at the same time, fear ripped a hole through her heart. For whatever reason, she trusted Jerry and agreed to meet with him briefly. More than anything, she needed answers. Perhaps Jerry was her only hope.

So, she sat alone, waiting for Jerry. Judith didn't want to admit it, but she missed Arthur. It pissed her off that he hadn't so much as sent a text message. Their trailer felt abandoned. The atmosphere was stale with lonely silence. Still, it was home. Judith actually came close to dozing off on the couch, until Jerry's Toyota Camry pulled up in the drive.

Jerry was a neat-looking man, short and chubby with reseeding black hair. His moustache and goatee were perfectly trimmed, and he always smelled nice. In fact, he was the opposite of Arthur, well dressed and well mannered.

"Hello, doll," he said, when Judith opened the door. She collapsed into his arms, embraced him tightly, and sobbed into his sweater.

"Are you okay, sweetie?" he asked, stroking her hair.

"No," she cried, with her glasses pressed firm enough into his shoulder to sting, "I'm not okay at all, Jerry."

"It's gonna be alright, sweetie. I promise. Can I come in?"

"Yes, please come in and talk to me."

He helped Judith to the couch and sat beside her. The lively, headstrong girl Arthur introduced him to six months earlier had withered into a weeping mess. Bruises the size of large fingers purpled across her throat. Her hair drooped oily and flat from a head, heavy with exhaustion and sorrow. Jerry was a natural nurturer; the kind of person who has hot cocoa waiting, when you come in from the cold and a warm bed snuggly made with fresh linens for you to sleep in at the end of a long day. Judith sprawled on the couch and let loose her feelings, as if Jerry was a therapist.

"Oh my God, it was so horrible, Jerry. I'm so scared."

"Judith, there isn't a person in this world, who wouldn't feel the same way. Honey, you saw a friend get murdered. It's okay to be scared and cry."

When Jerry held her hand, she didn't feel threatened like he was trying to make a move or manipulate her vulnerability. During the weeks Judith lived with Arthur at Jerry's house, they shared many hugs to celebrate joy or sooth disappointment. Not once did she see that look in his eyes, which indicated impure thoughts. She was well familiar with wolves. Jerry proved to be a lamb; someone she could talk to without worrying about being stabbed in the back or falling victim to ulterior motives. They became good friends and perhaps would blossom into best friends with enough time.

"What if he comes back for me?" she panicked, "What if this has made me crazy, and I have to spend the rest of my life in a padded room?"

Jerry placed a hand on each of her shoulders and turned her toward him. He smeared tears from her cheeks with his palm and tilted her chin up, so he could look her in the eyes.

"Judith, it's going to take time for the shock and fear to ease, but you're not crazy. You would be crazy if it didn't bother you at all. But I'm here to help you understand what you saw."

His comment kind of scared Judith. She held her breath and leaned away from him. It dawned on her that Jerry hadn't asked any questions about what she saw. He seemed to know, even though she refrained from giving an exact account to anyone. She told police that the perpetrator had a knife, but she knew he didn't. According to her statement, the man wore a monster mask. That was a lie. The murderer didn't wear a mask. Instead, he *really* was a monster. Jerry's lack of curiosity sparked suspicion.

"I want to show you a picture," he said, digging out his wallet. Jerry found a photo, crinkled and worn. He handed it to Judith. It was a snapshot of Arthur, wearing tacky clothes that looked like they were straight from the disco era. In the photo, Arthur proudly cradled a baby in his arms.

"That's Arthur," Judith smiled.

"Yes," Jerry confirmed, "and the baby is me."

She gave him a confused look that was almost angry.

"Judith," he continued, "Arthur is not my little brother. He is my dad."

Her expression did not change. Neither did she speak.

"I want you to relax and hear me out, okay? When I was a baby, not long after that picture was taken, my mom and dad went on vacation to Las Vegas. Dad has told me the story, but he doesn't go into a lot of detail. All I know is that, while they were there, a vampire confronted them. She killed my mother and cursed my father. He is a vampire."

Jerry waited for Judith to say something, but she didn't, so he carried on.

"Dad killed your friend last night in a fit of jealousy and bloodlust. But he is not going to hurt you. He came to me last night, pretty upset. We talked for a long time. He is willing to accept whatever the consequences might be, but he wants you to know the truth, and he wants you to know that he will never hurt you."

"Why did he look like that?" she asked, surprisingly calm, "he was a monster."

"Vampires are human monsters," he answered, "they need blood to survive, but what really sets them off is human blood. Dad can drink the blood of an animal and not become a monster like that, but if he goes after human blood, he turns into a tick. That's just part of the curse."

Judith began to cry again. She thought about the blood all over Arthur's face the morning they split. Whose blood was it? Her heart ached with the sting of betrayal. Judith prepared for what she thought was the worst- alcoholism or drug addiction. But who could possibly be prepared for vampirism? Yet the situation's absurdity didn't hurt half as much as Arthur's silence. She loved him so deeply, she probably would have accepted his condition and tried to help him, if he had only told her the truth.

"Dad's aging cycle is slowed down. It will probably take a few hundred years for him to look like an old man. Life has been tough for us. We've moved around a lot. It's hard to stay in one place when your son grows older but you do not. For a long time, we settled in the city. It's easier to blend in and find work there. But five years ago, I met somebody and as fate would have it, he lives here."

Judith gave him a strange look, although she didn't mean to. She had suspicions all along about Jerry's sexuality.

"You remember my friend, Todd? Well, he's more than just a friend. I think me being gay has oddly helped my relationship with dad. Both of us have a secret. Of course, they're two different kinds of secret, but nonetheless, it's helped us relate. After Todd and I got together, we moved here and just told everybody I was dad's older brother. But eventually, he will have to move again. Everyone in this town will age, but he will stay the same."

"I never saw him drink blood," she whimpered.

"He's secretive about the whole thing, as I'm sure you understand. There's a lady in West Virginia, which is where we are originally from. This woman is kind of like a vampire therapist. I know that sounds silly, but she's actually helped a few people in dad's position. They meet with her once a month and they can talk to her about things they can't tell anyone else. She supplies them with tablets she makes with animal blood. It's a sophisticated setup. The blood is tested for disease and everything. There is no doubt dad has been taking the tablets every day. He just hides it really well."

"Oh my God, Jerry, I think I'm gonna be sick. I need some drugs or something."

"Dad said he was so attracted to you, he couldn't resist going out with you. Then he fell in love. It's so hard for him because he wants love just like everyone else, but how do you tell your lover that you're a vampire? He wants to see you."

Judith stood, lit a cigarette, and walked around the living room in circles, letting the cigarette burn idly between her fingers.

"I don't think I can do that," she said.

"I understand."

Judith stopped circling and stood in the middle of the room, shaking. Her voice cracked as she spoke, nearly shouting.

"No, I don't think you do understand. Answer this for me, Jerry. Why did Arthur kill Arnold last night?"

"He just let his bloodlust take over. In all his years as a vampire, Arnold is the third person he's killed. Dad hates the bloodlust."

"Yes, but why did he pick Arnold?"

"He came here hoping to see you, and when he saw you and Arnold on the merry-go-round, he just flipped and went crazy."

"That's right," now Judith *was* shouting, "and I'm the one who asked him to take a walk with me. It's all my fault. I got him killed, Jerry!"

"No, you did not."

"Yes, I did!"

"No, you did not! Listen to me, Judith. Before this week, dad had killed one person. It was back when he first became a vampire. That murder has haunted him since then. For whatever reason, he's let his guard down and killed two people this week. I don't know what the deal is with him, but he has got to get it under control. When he came here last night, he would have killed Arnold regardless of if he was outside with you or inside with you. If he hadn't killed Arnold, it would've been somebody else. This is not your fault. It's dad's fault."

Judith sat at the center of the floor, slung off her glasses, pulled her knees to her chest, and cried rivers across her legs. Jerry crouched on the carpet in front of her.

"Come with me to my house," he invited, "You can chill out, and if you need to talk, I'll be there for you. What do you say? We can load up your things and go right now."

"I can't do that," she sniffled, "I can't see him right now. Maybe I'll want to talk to him again. I don't know. But I can't see him right now."

"Okay, I'll keep him away. I promise."

"No, Jerry, I can't. But please stay close to the phone incase I need you."

"Okay, sweetie, whatever you need just let me know."

After a long crying spell, Judith stretched out on the couch. Jerry found a blanket and tucked her in.

"I'll be back tomorrow to check on you," he promised, "Call if you need me, okay?"

Jerry left and loneliness gripped Judith instantly. For days, she ached with questions. Now, she ached with answers. It was a pain Judith knew would last forever. Leaving the lights on and the TV blasting, she slipped into sleep with one thought on her mind... maybe she should have gone with Jerry.

3.

The sun sat and RJ was gone. He had no desire to tell the sheriff hello and Amber goodbye. When Kurt called giving Amber notice that he was about two hours away, RJ ordered Benjamin to pull the limo around front. He did not say where they were going or how long they would be gone. However, she figured that was the last she'd ever see of them.

Amber cried non stop all day. Instead of feeling excitement for a new beginning, she quaked with fear and dread that the end approached; the end of happiness, smiles, life, and love. In her head an electric guitar squealed a patriotic sounding song that she did not recognize. Kurt had a lot left to learn about Amber, and that scared her. As far as she could see, good looks and wild sex were her only positive traits. He already knew about those. So, everything left to learn was negative. Amber regretted what she was about to put him through. Her boxes were stacked on the walkway. She sat on the front steps with arms crossed over knees and her head resting on top, when Kurt's headlights finally cut through naked trees on his way up Muddy Mountain.

He bolted out of the truck, clumsily staggering on legs cramped from hours of automobile travel. His pants were crooked; his jacket and derby lopsided. Rushing across the yard, he pulled his pistol from its holster, causing Amber to fear that he might shoot her.

"Where's Rockhouse?" he snarled, nearly sprinting.

"Gone," she nervously responded, "he left with Benjamin about two hours ago."

"Damn," he shouted, "we might be too late. Listen, Amber, we don't have a whole lot of time. Tell me, do you know necromancy?"

"I know some of the spells..."

"You've got to teach me how to do it."

"What?" she laughed, "It's very complicated. You can't teach someone in five minutes."

"Well, you're gonna have to."

"What's wrong with you?"

Kurt slid the pistol back in its holster and sat beside her on the steps. She looked like a girl waiting for the school bus. A red toboggan covered her scalp. Hands, concealed in mittens, jutted from pink sweater cuffs, which jutted from brown leather jacket sleeves. Her blue jeans, however, were ripped at the upper thigh, exposing skin. Fringy, pink and white boots swallowed the hems. Kurt could tell she had been crying.

"Sorry, Amber, I don't mean to freak you out. It's just that I got some news today, and I'm afraid another terrible crime is going to happen if I don't act soon."

Amber nodded sadly.

"I talked to your uncle today."

"My uncle?"

"Yes, RJ's brother, Randy."

Her mouth hung open and her eyes spread wide like she was choking.

"You talked to Randy?" she coughed.

"That's right. Listen to me. Tomorrow is more than just RJ's 100th birthday. He has a plan. I guess the rules of witchcraft will allow him to resurrect himself tomorrow. So, he is going to kill two innocent people and put his spirit in the man's body and his wife's spirit in the woman's body."

"Oh my God," she shrieked, "so, you do believe me. You believe I'm a zombie!"

"I believe you," he grumbled, "but that's not the point. Amber, he's been waiting his whole life for this moment. It's probably what has kept him alive so long. If he doesn't get to go through with this, he won't last another day. He'll just give up. And if he dies, you know what happens to you, don't you?"

Again, her mouth draped and eyes spread.

"Oh my God, I'm going to die."

"Not if his plan works. You see, he'll be transferring his spirit from one host to another. So, he'll have renewed life and so will you. But, Amber, the only way that can happen is for him to murder two, innocent people. I've been tearing my brain apart over this, and the only answer I can find is for me to learn necromancy so I can bring your spirit and body back together."

Amber did not cry or blink. She sat calm and still, in shock.

From the valley, town's lights twinkled like tiny stars. On the mountain, darkness swallowed everything. The gallant moon tried to provide a small glimmer, but only succeeded in furthering shadows. In fact, Muddy Mountain's shadow unfurled for miles. The abysmal black amazed Kurt. He never realized it before, but town was trapped within a shadowy shroud, not cast by a mountain or gothic mansion, but rather a frail, petite old man. The woods came alive with sounds of movement; rustling leaves and snapping twigs. A coyote howled, close enough to sting Kurt's ears.

"Kurt, there's something you've got to understand about witchcraft," said Amber, ignoring the coyote, "The spells are easy. They're basically nursery rhymes written for the purpose of invoking the fates. But making a connection is the hard part. To do something complicated like necromancy takes Zen-like concentration. Wizards spend a lifetime trying to perfect it."

"Can't I at least try it? Amber, baby, please, this is killing me."

"You're not the one who's going to die," she scorned.

"No," he answered, "but I am the one who will have blood on his hands, when the time rolls around and I let RJ murder those young people so I can keep you."

Amber looked at him. A tear broke free and trickled down her nose. Kurt hadn't cried since his parents' funeral, but at that moment, he teetered on the verge of tears. Amber's heart melted, seeing him sitting there, sporting his rugged jacket and derby, with the star of justice barely shining amidst Muddy Mountain's dense darkness, while teardrops balanced at the tips of his lashes. She gripped his hand with her mitten and stood.

"Follow me," she ordered.

They trotted across the yard through grass, muddy with melted snow. The desperate moon struggled to light their path. In the eastern woods, a coyote bellowed. Its lover answered from the western side. An orchestra of howls trumpeted through the hollows. At least a dozen Hell-hounds joined together in dreary song. Kurt kept a hand propped on his pistol.

"Where are you taking me?" he asked.

"To the backyard. There is something I need to show you."

She led him to the brick wall extending from the mansion's rightwing. About a third of the way down the wall, Amber had a makeshift step-latter built out of cinderblocks.

"I don't know why Big Daddy wanted this freakin' wall here," she complained, "but I hate having to go all the way through the mansion to get from the front yard to the backyard. So, I built me a little bridge. Be careful crossing the wall. It might be icy."

Amber climbed over first. Kurt placed his hand on her butt to help steady her over the top. He didn't have to do that, but it was very satisfying. The pistol pinched his manhood, as he scaled bricks. Other than that, he crossed with no worries.

"Like I said," she instructed, once they were on the other side, "the spells are easy. Concentration is the hard part. I've been trying the same necromancy spells RJ uses, but I can't make any of them work."

The mansion seemed endless. Pastel patches, painted by Amber, faintly glowed. Unpainted areas were dark with shadow. The contrast made the mansion appear deformed and misshapen like an abstract picture. Stick-figure trees with serpentine branches blocked what monstrosities watched from forest black, beyond the backyard. The air felt artic. Their breath wafted in opaque plumes toward the ghostly moon. Kurt detected a thousand sounds- leaves crunching, beasts grunting, owls hooting, and hearts beating. Coyotes lingered close enough to hear them panting.

"Amber, have you killed somebody?"

"No," she cackled, "but I have tried resurrection. Kurt, a skilled necromancer can place a human spirit in a coyote or even a machine. The possibilities are limitless. All it takes is the invocation of a spirit and the proper command for it to inhabit a host where no spirit currently resides. But the experiment can go wrong, baby. That's why there are hundreds of zombies executed every year. This kind of thing can really, really go wrong."

"Amber, just tell me the spell."

She rose onto tiptoes and whispered in his ear.

"Early to death, later to rise, give Amber's spirit this human disguise. So mote it be."

"That's it?"

"Yes. You can substitute amen for so mote it be if you want, but the spell will not work unless you close it with those words. That's important, Kurt. You have to say so mote it be. Other than that, just spill a drop of your blood on the body you want my spirit to possess."

"It can't be that easy."

"It's not. Haven't you heard anything I've said?"

Kurt thought he saw a shadow cross one of the second story windows, just as the cold breeze blew. In that moment, he realized for the first time what kind of life Amber had lived. Kurt loved her, but she scared the shit out of him.

"Amber, honey, why did you bring me to the backyard?"

"To see if you can do the spell I've failed to master. Come with me, please."

Frozen grass crunched loudly like bursting graves, as they continued toward the black mouth of wilderness, across the lawn. The backyard was another dimension. Slivers of fog resembled floating spirits. Owls screeched with demon voices. As silly as it seemed to him, Kurt could have sworn that the wind was blowing backwards.

"Do you see that mound of slushy snow over there?" Amber asked, pointing to the decaying frame of her snowman.

"Yes," Kurt acknowledged.

"Bring it to life," she commanded.

He did not reply with words, but rather an arched brow that spoke clearer than the most articulate tongue.

"I went walking in the woods," she explained, "and found a fallen creature. I brought the body back here and placed it inside a snowman. For days I've tried to bring the snowman to life. Now, it's your turn."

"This is ridiculous," Kurt cried, "It isn't going to work. I'm just gonna have to let RJ kill these people. I'm not Superman. I can't save the whole world."

"I think you should just let me die," Amber said somberly.

"Amber, shut up."

"I'm not supposed to be here, Kurt. I'll never be right until I'm dead. Are you ready for something like that in your life?"

Kurt stomped to the snowman's remains. He eyeballed it like it said something to insult him. Then he turned back toward Amber and angrily put his hands on his hips.

"I want you to know something," she confessed, walking toward him, "but I don't know how to tell you. Kurt, you should stop RJ and just let me die. I'm cursed."

"It's too late now," he replied, "You've done gone and cursed me, too."

Amber pulled off her toboggan. Hair spilled around her face

and bounced off her shoulders, collecting little icy beads of crystal from the breeze.

"I can't feel the cold," she whispered, touching his face, "You make me numb."

The wilderness halted its wicked chants, and all became silent, except for their beating hearts. Kurt wrapped his arm around Amber's small shoulders, gave her a loving kiss on the lips, then stared deep into her eyes and playfully placed his derby on her head.

"I've always wanted you to wear that for me," he admitted.

"Kurt, there's something I've got to tell you."

"Then why don't you just tell me."

"I don't think I can be with you."

"What? Why?"

"I can't bring the snowman to life."

Like a man drunk with frustration, Kurt stepped wildly, left then right. Vapor lifted from his head, hot with anger. Pulling his pistol and waving it in the air, he yelled.

"Will you stop being so cryptic? I know you're a zombie, but not everything is a riddle or spell."

"You don't understand."

"No, I don't, Amber. I don't understand at all. You're a walking contradiction."

"The snowman was supposed to help, but instead it's gonna kill everything."

Kurt's face purpled. He snarled and cussed. The point of eruption was near. Howls returned, this time indicating that coyotes had formed a half circle through trees at the backyard's border. They were now close enough to run Kurt and Amber down, should they try and escape into the mansion.

"It's a snowman, Amber. Even if you did bring it to life, it would just melt in a few days. What are you gonna do, lock it in a freezer? Nature wants it to melt because it is a freakin' snowman!"

In a wild rage, Kurt fired a shot into what was left of the snowman's breast. Howls transformed into whimpers, with the sound of gunfire, and terrified paws could be heard sprinting deep into the forest from every direction. The snowman crumbled, and as Amber said, a creature lay hidden inside. Kurt never imagined the creature to be human. He certainly did not expect that a simple gunshot into the gut of his girlfriend's snowman would reveal the lifeless body of his long-lost brother.

EJ tumbled to the grass and laid on his back with arms spread in "t" formation. His right arm stretched forward, the outline of pit bull visible on the bicep. With eyes closed and face well-preserved, he appeared to be sleeping. Kurt dropped his pistol and almost fell over with the first piercing blow of grief. He staggered to EJ's body. There could be no mistaking the identity- the tattoos, the scar on his chin from a childhood bicycle crash, even the smug expression on his face- everything looked exactly the same as the last time EJ walked out the door. But his chest did not move. His pulse did not beat. EJ Bochester was dead.

"No," Kurt sobbed, falling to his knees beside EJ's body, "I'm so sorry. This is my fault. How could I have been so stupid?"

Kurt couldn't take his eyes off the corpse. He wanted to hold EJ in his arms, but was afraid that touching the cold skin would make all of it real.

"You killed him," he cried, still staring at the body, "You're a monster. I should have killed you, you freak. This whole messed up family deserves to die."

Kurt stood, but before he could turn around, the pistol popped. A bullet hit him between the shoulder blades on its way through his heart. Blood baptized EJ's face, as his big brother tumbled dead across him.

"No," Amber screamed, dropping the smoking gun, "Kurt, don't die, please!"

She stumbled about the yard, still wearing Kurt's derby. Anxiety knocked her down on hands and knees. Through mud she crawled to Kurt's side, blood seeping from his fractured heart.

"Kurt, baby, don't leave me," she pleaded, "I got scared and had a panic attack, but I didn't mean to hurt you."

She shook his body but there was no response. Moonlight glinted off his marble eyes. With tears gushing, she rested her forehead on Kurt's cheek, already turned cold.

"I didn't kill your brother," she sadly moaned, "I just found his body back in the woods, almost in the same place where RJ found me. He looked so peaceful and young. I thought I could save him. So, I brought his body back here and put him in a snowman. He was so heavy. I almost broke my back, pulling him here. Everyday I did necromancy spells, but none of them worked. He just wouldn't come back. Then I met you and found out he was your brother. All I wanted was for you to be happy and not hurt. So, I tried even harder to bring him back, but time just ran out on me. I'm cursed to kill everything that makes me happy."

Amber cried and cried; her tears springing from a bottomless well. The lonely mansion creaked in winter's whispering wind. While Amber grieved, two brothers rested in eternal slumber, atop a mountain made muddy by water from weeping. Amber stroked Kurt's hair and closed his eyelids. Knowing that he was dead, but hoping he could hear her, she sorrowfully whispered in his ear.

"Je veux mourir maintenant."

4.

In the seventy-five years since Lola Rockhouse's passing, she never appeared in her husband's dreams. RJ longed for dreams of his wife, for he knew they were the closest he could come to a manifestation of how she used to be. His desire remained unquenched for three quarters of a century, until two nights before his 100th birthday, when she came upon him like a whisper. In RJ's dream, he was a soldier in battle. A bayonet pricked him, and he shivered on dew-moistened ground as blood seeped from his gut by the gallons. When first Lola appeared, he did not recognize her. She wore the same bridal gown from their wedding day. It remained pure white, even as she glided through the mud and blood coating the battlefield. Her skin was the same shade as her gown, but her hair was so vibrant with crimson, one glance upon her curls singed the eyes. When RJ, who was a young man in his dream, realized who stood before him, he began to weep so fiercely he could not breathe.

"Stubborn man," she whispered, touching his wound, "what have you done?"

RJ mustered enough composure to grunt out what he wanted to say.

"Lola, don't leave me. Stay here with me, please."

The mortars exploding all around paled in comparison to the fire in her eyes. Her hair danced in the wind of cannons, but her gaze remained on her fallen husband. Lola's preserved beauty limbered the bayonets and numbed the sting of bullets buzzing from the bunkers with improvised kinetics like bees with broken wings. She looked upon RJ with lulling peace, the same look she had given just after making love, right before sleep assumed primary seduction. Although Lola's beauty had never been more enchanting, the pale glow of her complexion and the thin crescent of black beneath her eyes eerily highlighted the looming of death. She was not alive. To say she was a zombie would be a morbid exaggeration. Equally exaggerative would be the claim that she was a ghost. RJ could not find the spiritual species to which the image he cradled in his arms belonged. However, one thing was for certain. Lola was not mortally alive. She could walk no further with him than the border of his dream.

"Why haven't you come to see me?" RJ wept, "It's been seventy-five years."

"Silly bones," she giggled, "it isn't as easy as you think. It is more difficult for the dead to walk in the land of the living than it is for a fish to abandon water and walk upon the sand."

"But you're here with me now," he answered, gently touching her cheek, which felt so real and so cold.

"Yes, darling, I am here now because it is almost time for us to be together. You have suffered so much. I do not want you to suffer anymore."

"When I am with you, Lola, the suffering will be over."

Then it ended. There was no dramatic kiss amidst the smoke of cannons. RJ's conscious snapped awake, preempting the chance for an emotional goodbye or 'I love you.' He lay in bed, shivering and nearly driven to tears once the realization sat in that he had awakened and left Lola behind in the land of dreams. Seventy-five years spent impatiently awaiting his wife's message from the grave had finally come and gone as quickly as a casual passing in a crowded train terminal.

Until Amber came along, a lot of folks in town assumed RJ Rockhouse was dead. Benjamin's cryptic vagueness only heightened conspiracy theories that the old man in the mansion was either murdered or just killed over, and probably got cremated in the furnace or buried beneath an unmarked mound in the backyard. Less than half a dozen people could remember seeing him on the streets of town seventy-five years ago. Those who believed him to still be alive labeled him a hermit. Rockhouse, however, was not as reclusive as rumor suggested. He, by no means, held an active social schedule. Yet there were a few witchcraft enthusiasts he visited from time to time, all of whom lived a long way from town.

Although RJ possessed capability to chill the atmosphere and paralyze the largest of men with fear, he could also be rather warm and friendly, whenever the mood struck him. Rockhouse occasionally lent such graces to Benjamin and Amber. Not even a man with a heart made of ice can be cold all the time. Even so, relationships never meant as much to RJ as his agenda. That is why he regretted resurrecting Amber. He cared for her; maybe even loved her. But he could not give her the nurturing she needed because her emotions did not matter as much to him as practice of his craft. Of course, it was not simply the craft itself that fueled Rockhouse's obsession. His love for Lola and desire to be in her arms again controlled everything RJ did. Immeasurable love turned him unimaginably cold.

With Amber there had been mostly silence underscored by friction. They felt reluctantly bound to each other. RJ accepted responsibility for Amber's problems. And he fostered a little bit of concern for her happiness, until the night before he turned one hundred. On that night, care for anything, except the spell that would reunite him with Lola, was tossed aside. Amber would not have understood. That is why he never told her about his plan. Benjamin, on the other hand, connected with Rockhouse better than anyone, since Lola's death. He wasn't much of a conversationalist, and Rockhouse figured him to be the victim of slight mental illness. Regardless, he understood RJ perfectly. Benjamin devoted his entire existence to serving his master's plan for resurrection.

The evening before Rockhouse's 100th birthday, while Kurt and Amber bickered over the spiritual significance of a snowman, Benjamin drove the highway outside of town, killing time, as his master commanded. RJ fidgeted in the backseat, hardly able to fathom that the moment he worked for most of his life was merely hours away. Feeling restless, Rockhouse did something rare. He struck-up conversation with his butler.

"Benjamin, I know we've talked about this, but I want to make sure you are clear. Tomorrow, I will be dead. It doesn't matter that my spirit will live on in somebody else. RJ Rockhouse is going to die and we will never see each other again."

Benjamin made no motion. He simply stared ahead at the road. Yet RJ knew he heard every word.

"I've made a will. Amber will get a little money. You're going to get some money, too, and the mansion. You can do whatever you want with the house- live in it, sell it, burn it down- I don't really care. The rest of my money is going to Arthur Addler. Don't worry about any funeral arrangements. I'm not going to have a funeral. My attorney will take care of my disposal."

Benjamin's shoulders sank and his head sort of bowed. It was the closet Rockhouse had ever seen his butler come to displaying emotion. Porch lights shined from homes scattered on the hillside. The limo passed at the precise speed limit, fifty-five miles per hour. To RJ, the world and everything in it seemed mechanical, including people. He thought about the robot nature of human beings- wake up, drink coffee, eat breakfast, go to work at nine, shuffle papers or shovel coal until five, go home, eat supper, watch television, turn on the porch light, and go to bed. In his perception, veins were nothing more than sophisticated wires, running from our carburetor hearts, so that the computers we call brains can receive programming necessary to keep us laboring throughout a useless existence. Yet most people live an entire lifetime, blindly believing that they are something special and the sun rises for only them. All the while, their lives are nothing more than routine schedules, forgotten within a century after their deaths, erased as if they never existed.

That is why Rockhouse connected so well with Benjamin. If ever a human robot existed, it was RJ's butler. He always drove the speed limit. Coffee, breakfast, and dinner did not come late or early. Benjamin ventured through an identical routine, day after day, year after year. However, unlike the rest of society, he never complained about it or expected more. He simply followed the motions like a well programmed robot. So, after twenty-five years, to see a hint of emotion from Benjamin intrigued RJ and touched him in an amused sort of way.

"If there's something you want to say, Benjamin, go ahead."

"Sir," he rasped, "I have nowhere to go."

Rockhouse sighed, shifted in the seat for a second, and then stared at Benjamin's eyes in the rearview mirror. He probably could have ended the conversation right there and Benjamin would have remained quiet, not demanding an answer. But for the first time in ages, RJ felt giddy. He actually wanted to help the dumb goon.

"I know you don't," RJ admitted, "but let me give you some advice. I'm leaving you enough money to buy a good looking wife and lots of friends. But be careful because they'll try to take advantage of you. Always make sure that your money controls them instead of them controlling your money. And this is important, Benjamin, so listen closely. If you do fall in love with a good looking woman, do not marry her without a prenuptial agreement. She might argue with you and threaten to leave you, but trust me, she's only bluffing. Before you get married, call Franklin Bates in Lexington and tell him that I advised you to get a prenuptial agreement."

There was no reply. Rockhouse wondered if Benjamin was smart enough to comprehend anything outside of the daily routine that ruled his life. Greatness rests on the shoulders of idiots. As phenomenal as RJ's resurrection would be, none of it could happen without Benjamin. He took care of RJ, at least until Amber came along. Old age isn't easy. Simple sicknesses- congestion, vomiting, diarrhea – are hard to shake. Almost anything can kill you when you're so close to death. The most difficult part of RJ's plan was staying alive long enough to reach one hundred. Benjamin and Amber increased the odds of that occurring. Of course, as much as Amber did to keep Rockhouse alive, she exceeded trying to kill him with stress. If not for "the clock law", she most likely would have abandoned him all together. As pathetic as RJ perceived it to be, Benjamin was his only friend. He knew more about his master than anybody.

"Benjamin, you've been a good butler and, sadly, my only true friend. So, I'm going to tell you a secret about me that people have wanted to know for years. I'm going to tell you what happened to my wife's body."

They were now deep into the county. The speed limit dropped to thirty-five miles per hour along the narrow, curvy road. Like a strobe light, the moon flickered through naked tree branches, as the limo scooted by. Those trees knew many secrets- love affairs, drug deals, and even murders. Tonight, they would hear the greatest of them all.

"At Lola's funeral, I took her body out of the casket and carried it away on my shoulder. I put the body in the passenger seat of my car and drove away, leaving behind a dumbfounded and horrified gathering of mourners, a lot of whom were Lola's family and friends. Her father and mother were not pleased with this to say the least. Of course, they did not take any action immediately out of fear that I was homicidal within my grief. They thought I was crazy with sorrow, and they were right. Had they followed me directly, I probably would have killed them, even if they were beloved by my deceased wife. They showed up at the house three days after the funeral with police officers. There was a big scene. Looking back on it now, it's hard to believe that nobody got hurt. But I did not go to jail, and Lola's mother and father never truly knew what happened to their daughter's body.

I told them I had buried her out back and showed them a gravesite. They did not trust me. Once again, they were right. The grave at the far end of the backyard, which has now grown over and is unidentifiable, contains the body of one of my former butlers, who died during his services in the mansion. Despite their disbelief, the body in the grave was not exhumed. I think Lola's parents decided that it was best to believe she had been properly buried rather than find out the unsettling truth. For a third time, they were right.

Once I got Lola's body to the mansion, after the funeral, I placed her on a bed I prepared for her in the basement. You see, I had a plan to resurrect my fallen wife. When I was sixteen years old, I met a witch. We were lovers for a season. In return for giving my virginity to her, she taught me an ancient spell of necromancy. I thought that if I somehow summoned Lola's spirit, I could use necromancy to return it to her body. This plan made sense to me because for a few years before I met Lola, I dabbled in necromancy. My subjects had only been animals, mostly coyotes and raccoons my mother made me shoot, when they came prowling around the yard. But if I made it work on animals, I could surely make it work on a strong spirited creature like a woman.

So, I laid my wife's corpse in the basement and began the process of invoking her spirit, which is extremely difficult work requiring exhausting concentration. You see, Benjamin, most spirits do not want to be invoked. So, when you awaken them, they are very angry and can even be violent. Then there are other spirits who desire to come out and play, like the ones that are conjured on ouija boards. But those spirits like to play for a reason. They love trickery. It was important in my experiment with Lola that I invoke her spirit and nobody else's.

So, I labored for hours, and then I heard a voice, seeming to come from out of the walls all around me. It was the voice of my angel Lola. She told me to fill the bath full of water and place her naked body inside. As she commanded, I filled the tub and carefully laid her body in the water. Upon doing so, the bath water turned coal black. It was so dark it lost all transparency. I asked the spirit if it remained with me, to which it responded accordingly, once again from out of the walls. Before I began the resurrection ritual I asked the spirit about intimate details only Lola would know, to check and make sure it was really Lola and not a demon manipulating me. The spirit answered correctly every time. My heart leapt with joy. Lola and I would be together again, and the life that had been robbed from us would be restored.

I did the ritual, and once it was finalized, it did not take long for Lola's corpse to come alive. At first, it was a hideous display. The body convulsed and the breaths were so strained, I was afraid the veins in her neck and on her forehead were going to rupture. But the convulsing stopped after a minute or so and the breathing became controlled. Then the body arose of its own will and stood in the tub before me. Upon first glance into its eyes, I realized that I had been fooled. The zombie had a look of confusion as it analyzed its surroundings, as if it were seeing the world for the first time. Then, when its eyes met mine, there was no affection, but rather spite, shining from the hollow core of its deep pupils.

Immediately realizing that I had been tricked, I grasped the zombie by the shoulders with plans of drowning it in the bath water. But the demon was strong and hit me with a powerful blow across the brow, which left a scar that would still be visible if not for these wrinkles. I fell to the floor in a daze, and the zombie leapt from the tub, escaping into the mansion. I may have been unconscious for awhile. I do not know. But I do know that the zombie had ample time to roam from room to room. When I gathered my wits and stumbled through the mansion, debris was scattered everywhere. I found the demon in Henry's quarters. Henry was my butler in the days of Lola's death. The demon had crawled into bed with Henry and snapped his neck in two. She toggled his limp head back and forth in her hands like a toy, with a wicked smile cracking her face. When my shadow in the doorway caught her attention, she raised those dumb, black eyes only to find the barrel of a pistol pointing at her brow. In my shock and despair, I underestimated the power of that demon. It could have split me in two had it so desired.

The demon did not wish to kill me. Instead, it knocked me to the floor and sprinted with great speed out into the yard, still naked. I followed, clumsily firing shots to no avail. I followed her down to the ravine, where she proceeded to leap, with no hesitation, from the jagged cliff into the rushing waters of the river, far below. Lola's body has never turned up anywhere to the best of my knowledge. However, from that day on, the mountain has leaked water like tears. Throughout the years, the mountain's tears have choked away a lot of the vegetation, leaving nothing but mud. Eventually, as centuries pass, tears will melt the mountain until it is no more than a tiny hill."

As RJ expected, Benjamin did not respond. They drove on in silence down the lonely road, combing naked trees. Rockhouse trembled with excitement. Benjamin did nothing more than breathe and drive. They had a destination but no set route for reaching it. Rockhouse wanted to make sure that Amber and the sheriff were long gone before beginning his ritual of immortality. Seventy-five years of devout work and relentless patience could easily crumble with merely one second of careless miscalculation.

Rockhouse ordered Benjamin to cruise around aimlessly until 11:15 PM, and the faithful butler followed orders precisely. Forty-five minutes before RJ turned the big 1-0-0, Benjamin entered Sugarland trailer park behind the wheel of a lavish limousine, and stopped in the driveway of lot #1. If everything went according to plan, it would not matter if police or any of the neighbors spotted the limo, for there would be no crime to report. Rather than being kidnapped or murdered, the world would perceive Judith Page to be the luckiest woman in the world; the heiress of RJ Rockhouse's fortune. Judith's face, body, and name would live on. Her spirit was a different story. Heaven, Hell, or Purgatory prepared a place for Judith's soul, with the vacancy to be filled by midnight. The superficial world would gaze upon Judith's body and consider her to be alive; her changing personality attributed to the sudden accumulation of riches. It was a perfect plan.

There was a light on inside the mobile home; however, no car parked in the drive. RJ hoped Arthur fell for his manipulation and stayed away one more night. Benjamin left the car running and entered the trailer. Unbeknownst to the tenants, Rockhouse had an extra key to every home. Benjamin did not need the key. In her exhaustion, Judith forgot to lock the door. She remained asleep on the sofa, not waking one time since Jerry left her. Benjamin tiptoed across the living room, stealthily for a man of his girth. Judith slept peacefully, oblivious to her creeping fate.

Slowly, Benjamin lowered to his knees. With one fluent motion, he pulled the pillow from beneath her head and began suffocating her with it.

In that instant, she awoke; her screams muffled in cotton. Had Judith been ugly, she would have lived a long life. Her beauty, however, attracted too many wolves. She kicked, flailed, and gasped, but Benjamin overpowered her. Judith could see only blackness. Her dying thought was that Arthur had killed her.

With her lifeless body wrapped in a blanket, Benjamin hurried to the limo as sneakily as possible. On their way up Muddy Mountain, RJ cradled her dead head on his lap.

"Don't you worry," he whispered, softly stroking her hair, "everything is going to be just fine, my sweet Lola."

5.

Seven-thirty the following morning, Arthur sat in an empty train terminal. He'd been there all night, weighing the consequences of two options, over and over... kill Rockhouse, inherit millions of dollars, and hope that the new wealth convinced Judith to forgive him... or hop a train to Mexico and rid his loved ones of the misery that is a vampire. Peace for those he cherished only existed with his departure. So, he purchased a ticket and awaited the southbound train headed toward proverbial Hell. Whether he would try again to live absent of human blood or divulge entirely in lust of the fang, he did not know. Nothing really mattered anymore. Arthur lost everything he loved, and he had a thousand years to think about it.

He left Jerry a note, simply saying goodbye, and instructing him to come get the Malibu. As much as Arthur wanted to see Judith again, he felt it best for both of them if he just disappeared. No belongings were packed and he had very little money. If worse came to worse, Mexican whores could supply nourishment until employment presented itself. As a vampire, Arthur was immune to all human diseases. So, whores could satisfy his lusts for blood and sex if need be. Arthur compared sucking a person's blood to having sex with a prostitute. While it's happening, the lust is like fire... the nastier the better... the high is intense. The moment it is finished, regret washes your soul. A bitter taste fills your mouth and thick filth covers your skin. It's never satisfying beyond the brief seconds in which it occurs. He hated being a vampire.

The seven-thirty train arrived surprisingly on time. Usually, no one got on or off. Occasionally, a few folks stepped out to stretch their legs or smoke a cigarette. Nobody wanted to stay in that God forsaken shit-hole. The train station sat thirty miles outside of town. There was one ticket booth, imprisoning a clerk bored nearly to tears. On the left stood an abandoned hotel/restaurant, with windows broken and cobwebs covering the doors. Other than that, nothing but raw wilderness could be seen all the way to the horizon. No one understood why they chose to put a train station there. The station did, however, make a great hunting ground for vampires. Lonely smokers could easily be snatched up, devoured, and buried deep in the wilderness. However, Arthur had no appetite that morning. He just wanted to get away.

The train looked sleepy as it groaned to a stop. Window shades sagged like heavy eyelids. With a snort, smoke plumed from the train's nostrils. Doors were yawning mouths stretching wide open with a loud sigh. One man stepped off. It appeared this was his final stop. A heavy duffle bag tipped the balance of his shoulders to the left. Humble, yet confident, eyes scanned the wilderness from beneath a floppy, brown derby. A dark, thin moustache curved with his lips, as he inhaled a gluttonous gasp of fresh, mountain air. With his wool jacket and brown leather boots, he resembled a man more accustomed to the western mountains. But he did not seem out of place. In fact, a look of joyful comfort consumed him as he peered about Appalachia. Arthur stood near the platform, giving his decision to leave one last consideration.

"Excuse me," the man called to Arthur, "are you boarding or exiting this train?"

"I'm getting onboard," Arthur answered.

"Oh," he chuckled apologetically, "would you mind telling me where I might find a taxi, sir? I'm in an emergency situation and there isn't much time."

"I tell you what," Arthur said, with a matter of fact tone, "that white Malibu over there is mine. The keys are in it. You can have it if you want."

"I'm afraid I'm going to have to take you up on that offer, sir. Thanks and God bless you."

He tipped his hat and strolled toward the Malibu. Arthur couldn't help but laugh.

"Wait a minute, man," Arthur called, "hold up. Look, I'm serious. You can take the car, but I have to know what kind of emergency has got you desperate enough to hop a train to this dump and then borrow a stranger's ride."

"My sister is in danger," he replied, "She is going to be murdered soon, if not already. You have trusted me with your car, and I promise it will be unharmed. You can find it parked at the home of RJ Rockhouse. He lives in…"

"I know where he lives," Arthur interrupted, "What is your sister's name?"

"Her name is Judith Page."

"Are you Seth?"

The man's shoulders popped flush and he arched an eyebrow.

"Yes I am."

Amusement left Arthur's expression and he became gravely serious.

"My name is Arthur Addler. I'm Judith's boyfriend. Hop in the car. I'll give you a ride."

Arthur wasted no time getting down the road. They were out of the parking lot before Seth had time to buckle his seatbelt.

"What is the old freak gonna do to her?" Arthur asked.

"Kill her," Seth replied.

"Why?"

"Rockhouse is a warlock. He wants to use Judith's body as a host for his deceased wife's spirit."

Suddenly everything made sense. RJ intended to murder him, too. When Rockhouse first proposed his plan, Arthur had no intension of taking him up on it. Then one moment of weakness sent the whole world into a downward spiral. He treated Judith horribly the morning they split, damaged her emotionally the evening he mutilated Arnold, and gave her the cold shoulder throughout a time when she desperately needed him. Even after Arthur admitted his mistake, he foolishly chose to try and buy Judith's forgiveness with cash rather than earn it with honesty. Now, his stupidity and weakness was going to get her killed. He couldn't handle the thought of her lying scared on a slab in Rockhouse's basement, calling out for him to rescue her. He refused to accept the possibility of her already being dead. Arthur knew in that moment he was going to kill Rockhouse, whether Judith was alive or not.

"How do you know all this stuff?" Arthur questioned.

"I do not know if Judith told you, but I have been serving as a missionary in China."

"Yeah, she read the letter you wrote."

"So, she got the letter? That's great. I was afraid it would never make it to her. If she read the letter, then you know about the old man, Max, who lived in the house with me."

"That's right… freaky dude in the attic."

"Yes, but it turns out he's a good person, very spiritual, in fact. He was trying to deliver a message to me, and I was too frightened by his appearance to understand. When Max was young, he came to America. He met up with RJ's brother, Randy, and was tricked into visiting RJ's house. He saw horrible things there and endured great torture. Randy Rockhouse used sorcery to turn him into a vampire."

"A vampire?" Arthur groaned.

"I know it sounds crazy, but you've just got to believe me on this. Max went through what he calls a cleansing ritual. This cured him from being a vampire, but it was the greatest tribulation of his life."

"Tell me about this cleansing ritual," Arthur demanded with more excitement than he should have shown.

"It requires the supervision of a priest or minister, although it is hard to find one willing to do it these days. But male vampires are castrated. They cut off most of his tongue, pull teeth and fangs from his mouth, gouge out his eyes and ears, and they have some way of corrupting his smell and touch. Basically, they take away the vampire's physical senses, rendering him nothing more than a blob of flesh."

"And this works?" Arthur asked, no longer enthused.

"It worked for Max. Decades of intense meditation have blessed him with great insight. He said he received visions of RJ Rockhouse murdering my sister in some kind of pagan ritual to be fulfilled on this day."

"If that old dude doesn't have any tongue, how did he tell you this?"

"He wrote it down in perfect English, even though he's never spoken or written a word of it. God's power is amazing. But I worry that I might be too late to save her."

"Not if I have anything to do with it," Arthur proclaimed.

The Malibu streaked down the highway, tires whining around every curve. Arthur displayed no concern for his passenger's life. Judith was all that mattered to him. Seth did his best to remain calm, whispering prayers with his eyes closed and head bowed.

Arthur's anxiety spiked to a level that probably would have given him a heart attack had he possessed the physical capability of experiencing one. He thought about Hollywood's romantic portrayal of vampires. How he wished those fairytales could be true. Then, instead of a hideous, pathetic coward, he would be a glorified bad boy, protecting his lover from the dangers lurking in shadows. In movies, beautiful women win the hearts of valiant heroes, and they live happily ever after. In real life, however, beauty attracts everything from heroes to worms, wolves, cowards, and monsters. Snagging a knight in shining armor from the mass of liars and manipulators is about as unlikely as winning the lottery. Judith Page certainly clutched a losing ticket when she selected him.

If any chance existed, Arthur would sacrifice his own life to save Judith's. Should both of them make it through alive, he would rid her of the misery that is a vampire, regardless of how passionately she begged him to stay. No matter how fast they zipped toward town, it seemed every mile took hours. The morning melted away, taking hope with it. There were three possibilities. They could arrive at RJ's mansion to find Judith alive. If so, God's grace prevailed. However, the other two possibilities presented Arthur with crippling sorrow. Judith's body could be dead, leaving Arthur damned to suicide or a thousand years of mourning. Then there was the likelihood of Rockhouse resurrecting her as a zombie. If they discovered her in such a state, Arthur would have no choice but to kill her.

A vampire and minister apprentice headed toward destiny in a streaking muscle car. For Judith's sake, Arthur hoped the apprentice's faith was strong enough to invoke Heavenly compassion because vampires are denied God's grace. Arthur knew if Judith's fate rested with his spirit, he'd see her lowered into the ground.

6.

Amber planned a ritual for her suicide. She wanted to die within the fantasy world that could have belonged to her, had she not been cursed to kill all hope. Originally, she planned to take Kurt's body along, but he was too heavy, so she stashed him and EJ in the woods near Big Daddy's wilderness trail. For the first time in her life, Amber drove a vehicle; the county sheriff's truck. It was a peaceful drive. She cried no tears.

At Kurt's house, she tossed his jacket on the sofa, along with the rest of her clothes. The derby remained on her head. Completely naked, she flipped on the radio, and danced through every room in the house. The cupboard concealed a sparkling bottle of champagne, waiting, perhaps, to uncork on their wedding day. Amber popped the cork and drank straight from the bottle.

"Ain't No Sunshine When She's Gone..." What a goddamned appropriate song for the radio DJ to play at that moment in time.

She cranked the stereo full-blast and made her way to the bedroom. Picturing him there, still in his tux, she swayed, naked except for the derby. Champagne sloshed in her left hand. The right hand held a secret behind her back; Kurt's pistol, still four bullets strong.

The blankets made serpentine motion as Amber slithered beneath. Stopping at the spot where his cummerbund would be, she undressed him in her imagination. Then she arose, blankets spilling from her bare shoulders. After guzzling a quarter of the champagne and tipping the derby toward his pillow, still dented from the previous night's sleep, she placed the pistol's barrel in her mouth and closed her eyes.

7.

On the morning of his birthday, RJ offered his body and two spirits as sacrifice. Standing before a mirror at the break of dawn, he primped and groomed, making his appearance pleasing for Beelzebub. The Gods prefer blondes. In accordance with their tastes, RJ transformed from decrepit old man into demonic young girl. A golden wig, made of real human hair, flowed from his cloak's black hood. Long, straight, radiant and beautiful, the hair looked alive. A porcelain mask covered his face, white like the moon. Black dove wings formed the mask's eyes. Frowning lips were also painted black. The cloak consumed his body like a shadow.

Curtains covered all windows in the gallery. One hundred lit, white candles circled the room. Judith's naked body rested on a scarlet sheet, spread on the floor in the circle's center. Hands were placed left on top of right directly below the naval. Her head was cocked to the side, with eyes closed and hair pulled back into a ponytail to show her face. Light flickered on her firm breasts. The candles' dancing flames cast shadows across the creases of her face and body, making her appearance even more voluptuous and seductive.

The air smelled of demons; burning flesh and smoldering ash. An odd hum seemed to come from the walls, soft yet eerie like evil monks in harmony. RJ approached the front gallery from the east wing hallway. As he passed doors, they rattled on their hinges. Ones not pulled all the way together opened, when he crossed. Those that were opened slammed shut, without anyone touching them. The cloak swallowed his feet, giving the illusion that he was floating. Short and frail, with porcelain mask shining in candlelight and sad eyes as black as death, he resembled the ghost of a little girl. The hum grew louder, as he seemingly levitated down the hall. Although Benjamin knew the vision to be that of his master, he still became frightened and exited into the kitchen, where sunlight splashed across the walls and the hum became muffled. Benjamin rarely drank alcohol, but on that morning he retrieved a glass from the cupboard intending to fill it to the brim with bourbon. His hands trembled so fiercely, he dropped the glass, shattering it on the floor. Staring at the broken pieces, Benjamin began to cry.

In the gallery, RJ limped along the inner circumference of circling candles. The mask's black eyes swung left to right like a pendulum, as he scanned Judith's naked body. Her skin remained creamy and full of color. She could have been mistaken for a girl, who had fallen asleep directly after making love.

All elements were perfectly aligned, except the most important one... Arthur's corpse. With RJ's host-body in place, all that remained was a simple, three paragraph spell, consummated by the traditional closing, "It shall be done. So mote it be!" Once those words were spoken, seventy-five years of tribulation would come to an end, as RJ and Lola reunited with an embrace. Overall, the spell would take less than two minutes. But without a host-body, sweet redemption might as well be a billion miles away. For three quarters of a century, RJ cursed the clock's slow pace. Now, he cursed it for racing so quickly. There was a short window of time, in which the spell could be spoken. That window closed another inch with each passing second.

Benjamin decided to lock himself in his bedroom and try to sleep through the incident. On his way down the west wing hall, he passed Lola's sewing room. During her brief time in the mansion, Lola spent summer days crocheting in a rocking chair, staring out the window, across town's lush, rolling mountains; her pet canary delivering a happy serenade from its cage, dangling in morning's bright beams of sun. After her death, RJ forbade anything in the room to be touched. Benjamin had only been inside a few times during his twenty-five years of service. Other than the occasions when RJ entered to mourn and reminisce, the door stayed locked and the room remained preserved like a tomb or a time capsule. However, the door stood wide-open, as Benjamin passed that morning.

Lola's yarn had disintegrated into frayed fragments, crumbling within an unraveling wicker basket. Books with yellowed pages and faded covers lined a dusty shelf to the left. Chocolate brown paint chipped from the walls, revealing drywall craters. The window caught Benjamin's attention. It was lifted halfway open. A frigid draft blew dust off tattered, blue carpet in plumes. Thin cloth strips, which had once been curtains, waved in the breeze like skeleton fingers. The rocking chair teetered back and forth in front of the window. A few days before Lola died, she completed a crocheted ataman, which still draped over the back of the rocking chair, although its tight weaving loosened with age and the brilliant colors had been bleached by the sun. Benjamin assumed Mr. Rockhouse visited the room that morning and left the window open. He would have ignored the situation entirely had it not been for the snowbird.

It perched upon the rusty remains of Lola's birdcage, chirping gleefully. To Benjamin the only thing more menacing than a bird in the house was a bat in the house, both of which he had experienced. So, he removed his jacket, hoping to shoo the giddy pest back out the window. Benjamin took only one step, and the snowbird fluttered from the cage and lit upon a dingy, bronze clock sitting at the bookshelf's corner. It flexed dirt-brown wings, mocking him. The clock was a small, wind-up model, with face so tarnished, Benjamin could not tell what time it stopped on. Corrosion robbed the bronze of all luster. Yet he knew better than to break it. If Lola had touched it, no one else ever could. He took one more step, and the bird did something bizarre. It began pecking the clock the way a chicken pecks feed. This act by itself would not have been extraordinary if the bird's pecking had not somehow brought the clock back to life. It steadily tick-tocked, and the rhythm maintained, even after the bird stopped pecking.

Benjamin calculated how he could capture the pest in his jacket without harming Lola's fragile timepiece. But the crafty creature once again burst into flutter, this time landing out of sight on the rocking chair's seat. Lola's ataman blocked view. Even with his impressive height, Benjamin could not see over the backrest. Slowly he tiptoed, jacket in hand. The rocking chair creaked... back and forth... back and forth. He noticed the breeze had stopped blowing, yet the chair continued... back and forth... its creak never slowing. The clock ticked loudly, reminding him of a bomb.

He cautiously approached, until finally able to see over the backrest's lip. A tiny, shriveled head bobbed, as the chair rocked; stiff patches of dead, white hair waving like cobwebs. Benjamin had seen enough supernatural apparitions in the mansion to become comfortable with the phenomenon. He tiptoed closer, in pursuit of the snowbird, unable to determine whether the image, limply swaying to and fro, belonged to a ghost or actual corpse. The body appeared solid. Yet there was no smell of decay. Its flesh was the color and texture of a prune. Lips curled inward along arid, toothless gums. Beige eyes, sans pupils, did not blink, staring out across town's mountains. Wrapped in white chiffon, the ghost/corpse cradled Benjamin's snowbird on its lap. A brisk breeze, wafting through the window, lifted chiffon from the corpse's body like angel wings, stretching to kiss Lola's tattered strands of curtain.

"Benjamin," a voice whispered from out of the walls. He recognized the voice to be his mother's.

"Mama," he gasped.

The corpse's left eyeball dropped in its socket so that the rotted iris pointed straight forward. Slowly, the shriveled head turned. Black slime oozed from its tongue. White chiffon, waving in the wind, opened to present a decaying naked body. A solitary maggot inched along the corpse's collarbone, following the chain of a gold necklace. Near the lumpy curve of deflated breasts, a heart shaped locket dangled, incasing the picture of a red haired, little boy, who Benjamin recognized as himself. Once again, he gasped, "Mama?"

Wrinkled, blue lips quivered, and thick, black drool spilled down the carcass's chin, as it moaned in agony, attempting to form words. Benjamin stared into its twitching left eye, trying to determine if the vision was indeed his mother's ghost or simply the prank of a mischievous demon. Tiny coughs cleared slime from the ghoul's throat, and with a gurgling voice it warned, "He's using you, Benjamin."

Bells on the resurrected clock began clanging excitedly, as if its alarm had been set for that exact moment. Benjamin dropped his jacket and staggered backwards. The bird quickly zoomed out the open window. Sobbing and clutching his heart, he stumbled into the hallway and slammed the sewing room door shut. Instantly, bells and gurgles hushed. The encounter confused him, yet Benjamin was quite sure that if the door reopened, he would see nothing out of the ordinary inside.

Meanwhile, Rockhouse continued circling Judith's body, thin fingers covering the black, dove-wing eyes of his porcelain mask. Tears seeped through wrinkled knuckles. Sadness struck him like Thor's hammer. The clock mocked non-stop... tick-tock, tick-tock. What a fool he had been to trust Arthur Addler.

However, well calculated plans always have backup options. Rockhouse preferred Arthur because of his youth and good looks. But he understood that Arthur might develop cold feet. Some people claim money is a curse, and this statement certainly held true for RJ's fortune. All names mentioned in his will served as possible subjects in his spell. Had Judith not shown, Amber would assume responsibility of hosting Lola's spirit. Rockhouse selected Benjamin as sacrificial substitute, in the event of Arthur's absence. RJ's daughter and butler never knew it, but they were pawns, all along.

"Benjamin," Rockhouse called.

The ominous hum sustained, its point of origin impossible to determine. It was the kind of noise that could be coming from miles away or inside your head. Rockhouse's call was welcomed relief for Benjamin, still shaken by his ghostly encounter in Lola's sewing room.

RJ slumped over Judith, examining her body like a piece of fruit or cut of beef in the grocery store. Beams of candlelight reflected below the mask's eyes, creating the illusion that RJ cried trails of fiery tears. Clasping the cloak shut with his hand, RJ walked to the circle's border, peering at Benjamin through a veil of smoke, as he entered the gallery.

"Do you hear that humming noise?" Rockhouse asked.

"Yes I do, sir," replied Benjamin.

"Don't be frightened of anything you see or hear this morning," Rockhouse continued, "I am making some powerful sacrifices, and that tends to get the spirits excited. But when my spell is finished, they will go away."

"Where is Mr. Addler?" Benjamin questioned.

"He'll be here any moment," Rockhouse lied, "I want you to help me make final preparations, so that when he arrives, everything will be in place."

"Certainly, Mr. Rockhouse."

"In my study there is a table with a stereo, a small gong, and a dagger on top of it. Please bring all of those things, including the table, to the center of this circle."

"Right away, sir."

The faithful servant was careful not to disturb placement of items on the table, as he carried it down the hall and positioned it in the center of the circle, according to his master's wishes.

"Thank you for everything, Benjamin," Rockhouse said, pulling a syringe from inside his cloak and jabbing it into Benjamin's jugular with one fluent motion. The butler's eyes rolled back in his head, as his body tumbled to the marble floor.

"I tried to get someone more handsome for you, Lola," RJ apologized, stepping over Benjamin's dead body, on his way to the table.

He started a CD, playing renditions of Paganini violin compositions, and sounded the gong, signaling the opening of his spell. Then he began to read aloud three simple paragraphs, which defined his whole life's work. With each word, the ominous hum grew louder, yet RJ's voice resonated clearly and commandingly throughout the mansion's halls. The hum reached a roar-like crescendo, as wind started to blow through the gallery, causing the candles' flames to expand and kiss, forming a perfect circle of light. Coyote howls echoed from the yard. The house seemed to sway. Nothing, however, distracted RJ's concentration. Once the entire spell had been spoken, he used the dagger to slice a gash in his left palm. He approached Benjamin first. After brushing hair away from Benjamin's eyes, he smeared blood across the butler's forehead. Then it was Judith's turn. Standing above the body, which in mere seconds would become Lola, an icy tear rolled through the wrinkles on RJ's cheek. Although the coyotes continued to howl and the mansion maintained its hum, he no longer heard them. Paganini owned RJ's perception; his violin bleeding sadness. If all went according to plan, after speaking the spell's closing, RJ's body would collapse, as the other two arose. The trickle of tears turned into a joyful flood, as he looked down upon his sleeping bride and began muttering the two short sentences that would wake her.

"It shall be done. So..."

The front door opened violently. Amber fired Kurt's pistol wildly in all directions. Hot wax splattered like melted butter across the walls, as bullets ricocheted through candles from off the marble floor. Had she aimed for RJ, she probably would have missed. However, one blind blast struck the hinge of his left jaw like a bull's eye and shattered it completely. As the mask crumbled, tiny shards of porcelain lodged in his eyes. He tumbled to the floor, breaking his fragile hip. Even amidst the pain, RJ attempted to form the last three words of the spell's closing (mote it be). Without these words, his entire life had been in vain. But the gunshot crippled his jaw and severed his tongue. All he could do was gargle blood. This effort, although persistent, would not be enough to appease the gods.

Amber stood above his broken body; Kurt's derby swallowing her crown, his jacket drooping from her shoulders. As she spoke, RJ's gurgles became angry growls.

"I want your dying thought to be this," she said, "you could have done good things with your life and spent eternity in Heaven with Lola. But now, you'll never see her again because she's in Heaven and you're going to Hell."

Amber walked to the hallway closet and locked herself inside. Oddly enough, she felt comfortable. Instead of having a claustrophobic panic attack, she relaxed like a baby in the womb. Her eyes closed, as her pulse slowed. She inhaled, exhaled, inhaled... exhaled... inhaled....... exhaled..... Then everything shut down. RJ and Amber died with the same breath.

Arthur and Seth arrived shortly thereafter to find bodies littering the gallery. Most of the candles still burned. Blood and wax speckled the walls. Seth whaled in agony when he saw Judith. After checking her pulse and realizing there was nothing else any human could do, he covered her naked body with his coat and began praying loudly in tongues.

Arthur's heart shattered with the sight of his dead lover. Since she was naked, he assumed her to be raped and possibly tortured before perishing. The thought of Judith calling out for help, as they bruised and penetrated her, completely broke him psychologically. He wanted to join Seth in prayer and promise God that he would go through the cleansing ritual, or even kill himself and every vampire he knew, if only Judith could be spared. Arthur wanted to pray, perform CPR, call 911, or just kiss her lips and cradle her in his arms. Instead, all he could do was turn and run out the door, sprinting across the lawn and well into the woods, hoping that Seth would not follow. The blood, coating marble in RJ's gallery, was human. One smell of it triggered Arthur's beastly transformation.

Arthur curled up on his side in a nest of tall sage grass and tried to prevent the metamorphosis. Yet the inevitable occurred. Skin mutated, as bones popped and reshaped. Pinchers protruded from his jaws and bloodlust consumed him like fire.

Arthur might not have been able to control nature's actions, but he held accountability over his own. Despite overwhelming hunger, he did not leave his little nest in the middle of the woods. There he stayed until the cravings subsided. Returning to the form of a man, Arthur cried loud enough for the sobs to echo. Yet neither human nor beast heard his sorrow. Winter drove all other creatures away. That is how life goes for the miserable vampire. Although he cannot die, everything else does, leaving him bound within an existence of loneliness, which slowly drags on for a thousand years.

8.

Then came the sun, touching everything like Midas. Temperatures steadied in the mid fifties, but it felt like eighty to the natives. Two hours after sunrise, town bustled, as if the blizzard never happened. All roadways were clear and alive with traffic. Patches of snow, which had not yet melted, were barely detectable along the mountains. The bright sun predicted winter's eventual fading. But six, fresh graves throughout town's cemeteries served as a reminder that, for some local families, winter would never end. Within one weekend, Arnold, EJ, Benjamin, Kurt, Amber, and Judith were lowered into the ground; sun bathing their faces one last time before coffin lids sealed them in eternal darkness. As for RJ Rockhouse, Franklin Bates arranged cremation of the body, in accordance with RJ's will. No one could offer any scientific explanation as to why the mountain, on which Rockhouse lived, turned muddy after his wife's passing. Neither could anyone logically define why the mountain began to dry, the day of RJ's cremation.

In the beginning, RJ was only guilty of loving a woman with all his heart. But like all things sweet, if left untended, love ferments. Rockhouse refused to let go and it poisoned his soul. He will forever be perceived as evil, and in many ways, this verdict is justified. However, as a young man, his heart was large and full of warmth. Nature cheated him, and he attempted to cheat nature in return. So, it is difficult to determine whether he was a perpetrator or a victim. Perhaps he is best labeled as a testament to how cold a heart can become, once it breaks.

It is only natural for folks in a small town to create legends, after a traumatic event occurs. The mass murder conducted that winter became known as "The Bloody Amber Massacre." It is ironic that the tragedy received such a name because Amber's corpse was the only one discovered without any blood whatsoever on it. The persecution Amber suffered during life paled in comparison to that, which she endured after death. The

"Bloody Amber" nickname resulted from belief that Amber massacred everyone discovered dead that week, before finally committing suicide. Although autopsies could not determine exactly what killed Amber, detectives agreed with the mass murder/suicide theory because the gun found beside her in the closet belonged to Sherriff Bochester, and it matched bullets in his body, as well as RJ's body. Technically, they could not prove that Amber killed Arnold, EJ, Benjamin, or Judith. However, lack of evidence did not matter. Everyone wanted an explanation so they could once again sleep at night. Since Amber was dead, detectives figured it best to tell everyone she lost her mind and was responsible for the whole, horrific display.

Thus, "Bloody Amber" was born. To this day, teenagers visit her unmarked gravesite, chanting insults in hope that such an act will invoke her spirit to pop out from behind a tree and say "boo!" Her image became representative of a monster, and her name became a curse.

No one knows whether or not Kurt would have won the election. Regardless, he will remain town's sheriff forever. John Spencer- the very man who wanted Kurt out of office- went on to win, and one of his first acts of business was to commission a statue of his predecessor. As long as town stands, so will Kurt, in front of the courthouse, his name and achievements engraved in bronze at his feet, along with two, simple words in quotations... "Our Sheriff".

Benjamin's burial was possibly the most depressing. There were no flowers, songs, prayers, or even mourners. Wanting to get the massacre out of everyone's minds as quickly as possible, the county government buried Benjamin. They did no research at all to see if he had next of kin, which was okay because, honestly, none of them would have cared. In typical government behavior, they cut every cost corner possible. The coffin looked like little more than a pine box. They chucked him in the same cemetery where prison inmates claiming no immediate family are buried, with a tiny, white, wooden cross serving as his grave marker.

The lack of immediate family proved beneficial for someone. Benjamin's inheritance disappeared into thin air, as did Amber's. There is no doubt that it landed in somebody's pockets, just not the pockets it was supposed to, according to law.

The bulk of Rockhouse's fortune, however, could not be

erased. For, the sole heir remained alive and well. The last will and testament stated that RJ Rockhouse, being of sound mind, did declare Arthur Addler a multi-millionaire. In Arthur's heart, he might have won the lottery, but he lost everything else. The only person, who wanted to die, was now the only one alive. Not even millions of dollars and a thousand years in which to spend it could ease the misery that comes along with being a vampire. Somehow, all of that stuff only made it worse.

Rockhouse passed something powerful onto his heir, but it was not money. Rather, Arthur inherited RJ's curse… a long life of trying to recapture a love, which is dead, buried, and never to return. Arthur understood this curse a little better than RJ did because Arthur had been cursed before. There would be no happily ever after. The only closure he could hope for was a tearful testimonial spoken to a mound of dirt. If Judith's spirit heard him, he'd never know it. Begging, crying, and praying solved nothing. She was gone forever. Yet, if tearful confessions over a cold grave were all he had to offer, nothing in Heaven or Hell could prevent him from doing so.

Arthur's shadow slithered across marble crosses. There might have been a hundred spirits watching in the cemetery, but he was the only living person there that afternoon. He stopped at the foot of Judith's grave, clutching a bouquet of eighteen roses, one for each year of her life. The dirt was soft enough to dig into, all the way down to her coffin. Flowers scattered across the mound, but not enough of them in Arthur's opinion. He knelt on one knee and laid roses at the center of her grave.

"I realize I never bought you flowers," he said. That was all it took to break the levy behind his eyes. Tears gushed, and he capped his mouth with his hand to keep sobs from thundering.

"I am so sorry, Judith," he wept.

He faintly heard children laughing, from a park down in the valley. Although Arthur could not see the children, he pictured them spinning on the merry-go-round.

"I will love you forever," he swore, "and forever is a long time for me. I don't know how to ask for your forgiveness because I don't think I deserve it. But if you ever want to haunt me in more than just my memory, go south of the border and find the most miserable creature in all of Mexico."

From the pocket of his trench coat, Arthur removed a cigarette lighter and a check for $487,000,000. He sat the check on fire and watched it shrivel to ash atop Judith's grave.

Walking off the hill, away from the cemetery, Arthur pondered the nature of monsters. Certainly he had become one, but what turned him that way; a demon's tongue or witch's wand? He concluded that curses and spells, although powerful, are not the most powerful forces in the world. A man is turned into a monster by his very own heart.

On his way to the Malibu, Arthur walked by the playground, where he heard children playing, while visiting Judith's grave. All of the youngsters happily engaged in various games, except for one. A boy, maybe twelve years-old, stood alone near the fence, staring up toward RJ's mansion, with an expression that could have been either concerned or relieved. As Arthur passed, the boy turned to look him in the eyes, holding the same countenance. A handsome lad with a bushy blond mane, cradling a basketball, and dressed for play, Arthur wondered what thoughts stirred in the boy's mind. His eyes followed every footstep. In the rearview mirror, Arthur continued watching. The boy limbered with relief, as the Malibu roared away, then dribbled the basketball; turning toward his friends and pumping his fist in the air, as if to say, "It is okay to laugh and play again, my friends, now that the monsters are gone."

About the Author

Sam Neace lives in Perry County, Kentucky with his wife and children. In the past three years, he has survived cancer, walked 500 miles, ran for political office, broke a world record, correctly solved a Wheel of Fortune puzzle before a single letter was turned on the board (at home, not actually on the show), and he authored the masterpiece thriller, Sugarland Melting. Sam likes long walks on the beach, candlelit dinners, romantic music, and scaring the hell out of readers. Saturday evenings from 7-11 PM, his radio show, Killer Radio, rocks the airwaves of WKCB 107.1 FM in southeast Kentucky and worldwide on *www.wkcb.com*. Visit *www.samneace.com* for anything else you want to know.

by Brad Parnell

Young Robert journeys to another world. There he comes of age amid a feuding government, grotesque monsters, an ancient ancestor ...and a couple of teenaged girls. With the help of a young wolf named Louie, Robert is introduced to the wonders and perils of a strange land called Gwerinatha. [Allegoric Celtic Fantasy, ages 12+]

by Ian Harac

One FBI agent
One geekette
One dead munchkin
Parallel worlds galore
An interdimensional conspiracy.
When Matt Anders stumbles across the body of a dead munchkin in a suspect's apartment, a conspiracy begins to unravel that leads him on a reality-jumping adventure to the magical Land of Oz... and beyond!
[Snarky SciFi Thriller, ages 14+]

Albrim's Curse

by Trevis Powell

All young Albrim wanted to be was a master bowman like his father. Then a savage attack on his home cost him his family, his arm, and his humanity – all at once! Crippled and contaminated by the Curse, his beloved Gran leaves him in the care of Mute, a giant warrior dedicated to protect-ing humanity from the depre-dations of the Quarg. Albrim does what he can to assist his master and redeem himself. But can a werewolf ever really recapture his humanity?
[Epic Werewolf Fantasy, ages 14+]

Gran's Secret

by Trevis Powell

Her son is dead; her grandson Cursed. Gran has to send him into hiding to protect him, and to protect others from him. But there are those who hunt Weres to use for their own evil purposes, and they are backed by the resources of kingdoms.
When these hunters begin snooping around Gran's village, there's nothing a sweet old lady can do to protect her grandson from such people, is there? Apparently, you don't know Gran.
[Epic Werewolf Fantasy, ages 14+]

The Veil

by Selina Fugate

A teenaged girl, Grace, draws the attention of an insane warlock. On the edge of death in a terrible accident, she makes a deal with Kracious, and is sucked into the warlock's sadistic game.

She meets a white witch that sets out to break her curse, but Kracious steps up the cat-and-mouse game with Grace's life to a new level.

Grace is suddenly shown the world behind "The Veil." A world with faeries, fallen angels, talking cats, and werewolves. A world she couldn't even imagine existed.

[Teen Fantasy Horror, ages 12+]

IMMORTAL BETRAYAL

by Paul Lewis

Darien, viking and explorer, braves the treacherous seas to discover new lands. That changes when he falls in love. But his world is shattered when he learns she has already been promised her to another. Darien's loyalty is put to the test as he battles vampires and werewolves. Darien finds himself having to choose between the woman he loves and his very soul. With tragic romance, heart stopping thrills, and plot twists, Immortal Betrayal aims to please.

[Tragic Fantasy Horror, ages 14+]

www.BlackWyrm.com